CHROMA

STORIES

Frederick Barthelme

SIMON AND SCHUSTER
NEW YORK

Stories in this volume originally appeared in *The New Yorker, Chicago Review, Kansas Quarterly, North American Review, GQ, New Orleans Review, Fiction, South Carolina Review, New York Arts Journal,* and *Playboy.*

Library of Congress Cataloging-in-Publication Data
Barthelme, Frederick, date.
Chroma.
I. Title.
PS3552.A763C47   1987   813'.54   86-31537
ISBN: 0-671-54255-9

For Andrew

CONTENTS

7

CONTENTS

CHROMA

DRIVER

Rita says the living-room lights keep her awake when she goes to bed before I do, which is most of the time. The light comes down the hall and under the bedroom door, she says, and in the dark it's like a laser. So on Sunday, after she'd gone to bed, I started to read *Money* in semidarkness, tilting the pages to get the light from a book lamp clipped onto the magazine. That didn't work, so I gave it up and watched a TV program about lowriders in San Diego. They put special suspensions in their cars so they can bounce them up and down. That's not all they do, but it's sort of the center of things for them. I'd seen the cars before, seen pictures of them jumping—a wonderful thing, just on its own merits. I watched the whole show. It lasted half an hour, and ended with a parade of these wobbling, hopping, jerking cars creeping down a tree-lined California street with a tinkly Mexican love song in the background, and when it was done I had tears in my eyes because I wasn't driving one of the cars. I muted the sound, sat in the dark, and imagined flirting with a pretty Latin girl in a short, tight, shiny dress with a red belt slung waist to hip, her cleavage perfect and brown, on a hot summer night with a breeze, on a glittering street, with the smell of gasoline and Armor-All in the air, oak leaves rattling over the thump of the car engine, and me slouched at the wheel of a violet Mercury, ready to pop the front end for a smile.

In the morning I left a note attached to the refrigerator with the tiny TV-dinner magnet, telling Rita what time I'd be home from the office, then got in the Celica and headed for the freeway. I'd been in traffic for half an hour, most of it behind a bald, architect-looking guy in a BMW 2002, when I saw a sign for Kleindienst Highway Auto Sales. This was a hand-painted sign, one quarter billboard size, in a vacant lot alongside the freeway—a rendering of a customized 1949 Ford. I got off at the next exit and went back up the feeder to get to this place, which was a shell-paved lot with a house trailer at the rear, strings of silver and gold decorations above, and a ten-foot Cyclone fence topped with knife wire surrounding it.

A guy jumped out of the trailer the minute I got onto the property. He followed me until I parked, then threw an arm around my shoulders before I had my car door shut. "Howdy," he said. "Phil Kleindienst. Hunting a big beauty, am I right?"

"Just looking," I said.

"We got the classics," he said, making a broad gesture with his free arm. He swung me around toward a Buick four-door. "Mainstream, high-profile, domestic, soon-to-be-sought-after classic road machines for the world of tomorrow."

"That's a big amen," I said.

He liked that. He laughed and walked me around the lot, keeping his hands on me the whole time—on my shoulder, my forearm, my back. He didn't have any cars that weren't huge and American, and he didn't have any custom cars. "Take a gander at this," he said, opening a brown Chrysler sedan. "This baby's autorama clean."

We went up and down the rows together. He was citing virtues, giving me histories, and I was looking for the hot rods. Finally, I said, "What about this sign?"

"What sign?" Phil said.

"Out there on the freeway," I said. I pointed back up to where the sign was. We could just see the back of it.

"Aw, you don't want to mess with that stuff. Lemme show you an Eldorado I got."

He started to move again. I said, "I'm a little late. I guess I'll have to come back another time. Thanks anyway."

"Hold your hanky there," he said. "I got one. I'll show you one. A Lincoln, pretty old."

He took me around beside the trailer to a corner with a banner that said "Bargain Corral" strung over the top. There was one car there, and it could have been in the TV show I'd seen. No price was soaped on the windshield, so I asked.

"Oh, hell," he said. "I don't know. Too much. Let's go back up front, lemme show you some sweethearts." He turned me toward the front of the lot. "How about this Caddy? About a '77, a honey-dripper. Purrs like a pistol."

I stopped him. "You don't want to tell me what you're getting for this one? What's the deal?"

"Whew," he said. "You're too tough. You're kidding

me, right?" He waited a minute, looking me over to see whether or not I was kidding him. "You don't want that porker, do you?"

The Lincoln was pale blue with black and green pinstripes, front wheels smaller than the rear, and it was low, maybe two inches off the ground. There was an airbrush illustration on the side, between the front and rear wheel wells—a picture of the Blessed Virgin, in aqua-and-white robes, strolling in an orange grove, behind each tree of which was a wolf, lip curled, saliva shining. The glass in the windshield and in the doors was dark green, and the steering wheel was huge and white. A head-bobbing metal Bambi—I think it was supposed to be Bambi—sat on the shelf behind the back seat, staring out the rear window.

I said, "I'm just curious. What's it worth?"

He let go of me for the first time since I'd arrived, backing away, putting a little distance between us as he studied the car. Finally, he slapped his hands together and said, "I don't even want to give you a price on that there. See, that's my boy Pico's car. Was anyway. Pico got shot up in Nam. He was this kid used to hang around, then worked for me. Built the car himself—did all the custom work, put in the hydraulics, stereo. All that in there's rhino skin. I don't even know where he got that."

"Looks professional," I said.

"Oh, yeah, heck yeah. He was good. He's got D. & H. Reds in there. It's real clean. It's about a thousand percent clean. He's got so much chrome under the hood you could put the hoses in your bathroom, use 'em for mirrors. I don't know why he's got these tiny wheels up front here, I guess that's a cholo thing. . . ." Phil gazed at the Lincoln. He was half-fat, maybe forty, with prickly blond hair, double-knit pants, a short-sleeved white shirt with a spread collar. "Pico cut her himself—know what I'm saying? Build a car like that today cost a fortune." He grinned and held his hands up as if giving me the bottom line. "I figure we're talking six, in the six area."

"What about the Toyota?" I said.

"O.K. Fine. That's all right," he said. "I can work with you on that." He locked an arm around one of mine and gave me a quick pull toward the office. "Let's boot some numbers around."

His trailer smelled like Pine-Sol. Everything was covered in knubby fabrics, earth tones. There was a dining booth, a tiny kitchen, a living space with a six-foot ceiling and a bubble skylight. He had four TVs, all consoles and all turned off, lined up against one wall. When we sat down, he said, "Let's verify our situation here. What's your line?" He was shuffling around, looking through a wood-grained-cardboard file cabinet.

I said, "I'm in sales. Pools, pool accessories, like that. Above ground stuff. Is that what you mean?"

"Naw. I mean how come you want this car? Is this a kick-out-the-jambs thing for you, or what?" He waited a second, then went on. "O.K., so don't tell me. What's your telephone? I'll check your wife on the deal. You got a wife, don't you?"

"Rita," I said.

"I mean, you tool in Nipponese and want to leave a Flying Burrito Brother, and I don't buy it. What's the better half gonna say? How do I know you got the bucks? How do I know you're in your right mind?"

"I don't know, I do, and I am," I said.

"Ha," he said. "That's good. What's the number? Better gimme the bank, too."

I gave him the numbers. He said, "Great. Get you something in the fridge. I got some Baby Ruths in there, if you got Olympic teeth. Help yourself."

He wiggled out from behind the table, went through a narrow hall to the rear of the trailer, shut a door between that room and the one I was in. There was a Plexiglas panel in the door, so I could see him in there, black telephone receiver to his ear, staring at the ceiling as he talked, swatting his hair with the papers from the file cabinet.

He was only in there a minute. When he came back he said, "The woman's not home, but the bank thinks you're aces." Then he gave me a long look. "Now listen," he said. He reached up under his shirtsleeve to scratch his shoulder. "I'm thinking you don't genuinely want this car. I know I'm supposed to be breaking your leg to sell it, but I figure you got some kind of momentary thing going, some kind of mid life thing—you look like you're about mid life."

I shrugged. "Not yet."

"Yet don't matter," he said. "My brother had his at twenty-seven. By twenty-nine he was putting toast in milk during the local news." Phil brushed something off the table. "Tell you what," he said. "I'll rent it. You take it maybe a day or two, leave yours on a collateral basis, take this guy, drive him a couple of days. Then, you still want it, we come to closure. How's that? I don't want you down my throat next week begging to undo the deal, right?"

I said, "I'll rent it right now."

"Sure you will," he said. "And I don't like it, but now and then, hell—what's it hurt?" He started through the file cabinet again. "I got a form here saves my heinie when you go to Heaven in it."

Phil had to go to his house to get the form. He lived right down the street, and he asked me to mind the store while he went, so I sat on the steps of the trailer and watched the highway. Traffic had thinned out a lot. He was gone forty minutes. When he got back I took the Lincoln.

I stopped at an Exxon station and filled up with gas, then drove to my office. I had just gotten into my assigned parking space when a young associate of mine, Reiner Gautier, pulled up in the drive behind me.

"What, you went overboard on chimichangas?" he said. "What is that? Where'd you get it?"

"Just trying her out," I said.

"You got a built-in Pez dispenser on there?"

I waved the remark away and pretended to search my briefcase, hoping Reiner would move along. Finally, I had to get out. He'd left his car door open and was giving the Lincoln a careful look.

"That's Mary," he said, pointing to the picture on the side of the car. "She's got wolf trouble there, doesn't she?"

I shrugged. "She'll make out."

He looked at the picture another minute, turning his head back and forth. "That says it all, know what I mean? I like it. I go for this cross-cultural stuff." He walked back toward his car, giving my shoulder a pat on the way.

I let him leave, then got back in the Lincoln and pulled

out of my space. I went to the shopping center near the office, stopped in the parking lot, and tried out the lifts. I looked out the door and I was better than eighteen inches off the ground. That got the attention of a black woman who was standing outside the ice-cream store, leaning against one of those phone-on-a-pole phone booths.

She said, "That some kind of trick car?" She was a young woman, in her twenties, and good-looking except that she was snaggletoothed. She was holding a clear plastic shopping bag with yellow rosettes on it.

I said, "Yeah. I guess it is."

She looked at me, then at the car, with a kind of amused curiosity, tilting her head back, squinting her eyes as she sized me up. "Well," she finally said. "What else do it do? Do it dance or anything?"

I grinned at her, shaking my head, then put the car in gear and left. At a bar called Splasher's, which I pass every day on my way back from work, I pulled up and went in for a beer. I'd never been in this bar before. It was one in the afternoon and the place was deserted except for a woman with feathery hair who handed me a wet bottle of Budweiser. She was cleaning up. The ceiling was falling in on this place. The walls were black, and the only illumination came from back of the bar and from the beer signs you always see, the kind that sparkle and throw little dots of light. One sign had a waterfall that light rushed over. I took my beer to a window table so I could watch the car through the stick blinds.

The woman played Country Joe and the Fish on the jukebox. I thought that was amazing. I spun my coaster, listening to this music I hadn't heard in twenty years. Between tunes I went to get a bag of beer nuts from a metal rack next to the cash register. The woman watched me search my pocket for change, then nodded when I put two quarters on the bar.

Two kids on trail bikes stopped outside to give the car a look. These kids were about fourteen, with dirty T-shirts and minimal hair. They straddled their bikes and stared in the car windows, and I smiled about it until I saw that the kid on the driver's side was prying off the door mirror. Then I rapped on the glass and went out. "Hey! Get off of that, will you?"

The kid who had been doing the prying gave me an innocent look. "Great car," he said. "We're checking it out. Right, Binnie?"

Binnie was already on the move, standing on the pedals of his bike, rolling away. "Pretty good," he said. "For a dork-mobile."

I said, "Sorry you're leaving."

"Whoa . . ." he said.

The first kid started moving, too. Then he stopped his bike and turned to me. "Hey," he said. "You know that mirror on your side? It's real loose. I can probably fix it up. Ten bucks."

I gave him a nasty look and shook my head, then got in the car. I stopped at a drugstore on the way home, went in to get cigarettes. A college-age guy with blue eyes and pretty brown hair was in back, sitting at a folding table, eating his lunch. It didn't look like takeout food—it looked homemade. He had a dinner plate, a salad plate, a jelly glass with red and green swirls on the side. There was milk in the glass. He asked if he could help me.

"I need a pack of cigarettes," I said.

He came across to the cigarette counter, wiping his mouth with a yellow paper towel. "What kind?"

I said, "True. Menthol."

He looked at his cigarette rack, one end to the other, then turned around and said, "I don't see 'em. You see 'em out there?" He pointed to the front of the counter, where more cigarettes were displayed.

I'd already checked, but I looked again. "None here."

He came out from behind the counter rewiping his mouth. "I don't guess we have 'em. I was sure we did, but I guess I was wrong. I can order you some."

I waited a second or so, looking at the guy, then picked a pack of Kools off the counter. "How about these?"

"We got those," he said.

Rita came to the window when I pulled up in the driveway and honked. It took her a minute, but then she figured out it was me and dropped the curtain. "What's this?" she said, coming out the front door.

I held up a hand and said, "Wait a minute. Stay there. Watch."

She stopped by the gas lamp at the edge of the drive. I jumped the front end of the Lincoln a little, then as far as it would go. Then I raised the rear to full height, then the front. I kept the car up until she was coming for a closer look, then I let it down, left front first, like an elephant getting on its knees in a circus show. That stopped her.

I got out of the car. "How do you like it?"

"Whose is it?" she said.

"Ours." I put an arm around her and did a Phil Kleindienst sweep with my free hand, covering the Lincoln front to back.

"What about the Celica? Where's the Celica?"

I reached in the driver's window and pulled the hood release, so I could show her the chrome on the engine.

"Traded it," I said, leading her around to the front. "Guy gave me a whopper deal."

She stopped dead, folding her arms across her chest. "You traded the Toyota?"

"Well, sort of. But this is a killer car. Look at the engine. Everything's chrome. It's worth a zillion."

Rita looked at the sky.

"C'mon," I said. I tugged her arm, leading her to the passenger side, and put her in the car. I went back around, latched the hood, then got in and started the engine. I waited, listening to the idle. "Amazing, isn't it? Can you hear that?"

"The motor? I hear the motor. Is that what you're talking about, that rumbling?"

We toured the neighborhood, then I started to go downtown, but Rita remembered she needed some lemon-pepper marinade, so we stopped at the super-market. I sat in the car while she went inside. A lot of people walked by wearing shorts, and all of them looked good.

We picked up a family bucket of fried chicken on the way back, ate most of it in the car, then finished up inside. Then we had bananas and ice cream. After that Rita switched on the VCR and put in a tape. "I want you to see this," she said.

It was a PBS documentary about China—about a peas-ant family. The grandmother ran things and got carried around on the back of a bicycle through this gorgeous countryside of misty, contoured land. Her son didn't know much about communism but felt things were a lot better now, with the Four Modernizations. His wife cooked, his daughters helped in the field, and his son wore a leather motorcycle jacket when he went out to help with the harvest. At the end they cut to the father, alone in some room, sitting by a big vase with thin branches in it, dusty light slanting in. He talked about the family, his voice ricocheting around the high registers while out-of-sync white translations popped on the bottom of the screen. When he got to his son, what he said was that the boy had been "stunned by the West."

That was it. Rita stopped the sound and we watched the credits go by, then the network logo, then some previews of WGBH shows. She poked me and pointed to the *TV Guide*, which was on the coffee table on my side of the couch. I gave her the guide and then watched her look up listings.

When she finished, she tossed the magazine back on the table. "Well?" she said.

"It's a rent-purchase thing," I said. I showed her the paper I'd signed for Phil Kleindienst. "I can give it back any time."

She laughed and said, "Hey! Not so fast. I may love it. I may want to go for a spin."

We went out about ten o'clock. It was cool, so we slouched down in the seats and left the windows open. We went by an apartment project we used to live in, and then we went over to the other side of town, where there is a lot of heavy industry—chemical plants and refineries.

Rita said, "It rides pretty good, doesn't it?"

"It's stiff when it's down," I said.

"So pump her up," she said. "I wonder what it'd be like to keep."

"People would stare."

"Great," she said. "It's about time."

She looked terrific in the car. She had on a checked shirt open over a white Danskin, her feet were up on the dash, and her short hair was wet and rippled with wind. Her skin was olive and rough, and it was glowing as if she were in front of a fire. When I missed a light next to Pfeiffer Chemicals, a couple of acres of pipes and ladders and vats and winking green lamps, I leaned over to kiss her cheek, but she turned at the last minute and caught me with her lips.

"Why, thank you," she said when I sat back again.

"Yes," I said.

On the way home we stopped at the mall. The stores were closed, but there were kids roller-skating in the parking lot, and a couple of cars parked nose to nose under one of the tall lights. We pulled up next to a palm tree in a planter about fifty yards away from the kids.

Rita said, "It's amazing out here, isn't it? How can this place be so good-looking?"

"Beats me," I said.

She put her head in her hands. "It's awful, but I have a craving for tamales. Really. I'm not making a joke, O.K.?"

One of the kids, a girl in shorts, pointed a finger at us and skated over. "How come it stays up like that?" she said.

"Just magic," I said. But then I opened the door and showed her, letting the car down real easy, then jumping the front a little bit for her.

"You've got her now," Rita whispered.

The girl stood back with her hands on her waist for a second. "Boy," she said.

She was pretty. Her shorts were satin, with little specks of glitter on them, and she had on a tiny under-shirt-style top. Some trucks sailed by on the highway. I offered Rita a Kool. She took it and held it under her nose.

"What's your name?" I said to the girl, rolling my cigarette between my fingers.

"Sherri," she said. "With an 'i.'"

I nodded. "You out here a lot?" I wagged my hand toward the other kids, who were sitting on the hoods of their cars watching us.

"Sure," she said. She rocked back and forth on her skates, rolling a little, then stopping herself with her toe. "Make it go up again, O.K.?"

I did that, getting it wrong the first try, so that I had one side up while the other was down. Rita was laughing in a lovely way.

The girl watched, then shook her head. "Boy," she said, smiling and skating two small circles before starting back toward her friends. "You guys are weird."

"Howdy," Rita kept saying all the way home. "Howdy, howdy, howdy. Howdy."

She went to bed at one. I couldn't sleep, so I watched a movie we'd rented a couple days earlier. When that was over I rewound it, paged through an issue of *Spin* that she'd picked up at the grocery store, then watched the end of a horror show on HBO. By then it was after four. I tried to sleep but couldn't, so I got up and went outside. It was almost light enough to see out there. I sat in the Lincoln and thought about how nice it was that Rita could just sleep whenever she wanted to. After a while I started the car and went for a drive. I stopped at an off-brand all-night market and bought some liquid refreshment in a sixteen-ounce nonreturnable foam-sleeved bottle. I wondered if the glass was less good than glass in regular bottles.

The scent of countryside in the morning was in the air. The rear window was smeared with condensation, and the storefronts were that way, too, and it was hard to focus on the stoplights, because of the way they made rings around themselves.

I went downtown, and it was like one of those end-of-the-world movies down there, with somebody's red hamburger wrapper skittering across a deserted intersection. The sky was graying. I made a loop around the mayor's Vietnam memorial, then took the highway running west, out past the city limits. The mist got thicker. Close to the road the trees looked right, but farther away they just dissolved. In the rearview mirror I could make out the empty four-lane highway, but above that it was like looking through a Kleenex.

Finally, I turned around and drove back by my secretary's apartment, saw her car with its windows solidly fogged, then passed the mall again. Some overnight campers had turned up in the lot, and their generators were chugging away. There were two Holiday Ramblers, cream-colored, squarish things, and an Airstream hitched to a once green Chevrolet. I pulled in and stopped. The air was so wet you could feel it when you rubbed your fingers together. The sky showed bits of pink behind a gray cloud that was big above the eastern horizon. A bird sailed by in front of the car, six feet off the blacktop, and landed next to a light pole.

These two dogs came prancing into the lot, side by side, jumping on each other, playfully biting each other's neck. They were having a great time. They stopped not far away and stared at the bird, which was a bobwhite and was walking circles on the pavement. They stared, crouched for a second, then leaped this way and that, backward or to one side, then stared more. It was wonderful the way they were so serious about this bird. These dogs were identical twins, black-and-white, each with an ear that stood up and one that flopped over. I made a noise and their heads snapped around, and they stared at me for a minute. One of them sat down, forepaws stretched out in front, and the other took a couple of steps in my direction, looked for a sign from me, then twisted his head and checked the bird.

The dash clock said it was eight minutes to six. I wanted to drive home real fast and get Rita and bring her back to see everything—the dogs, the brittle light, the fuzzy air—but I figured by the time we got back it'd all be gone.

The lead dog took two more steps toward me, stopped, then stretched and yawned.

I said, "Well. How are you?"

He wagged his tail.

I said, "So. What do you think of the car?"

I guess he could tell from my voice that I was friendly, because then he did a little spasm thing and came toward me, having trouble keeping his back legs behind his front. I opened the car door and, when he came around, patted the seat. He jumped right in. He was frisky. He scrambled all over the place—into the back seat, back into the front—stuck his head out the passenger window, ducked back in and came over to smell the gearshift knob. The other dog was watching all this. I called him, then put the car in gear and rolled up next to him. He didn't move for a minute, just gave me a stare, kind of over his shoulder. I made that kissing noise you use to call dogs, and he got up and came to the door, sniffing. Finally, he climbed in. I shut the car door and headed home. They were bouncing around, and I was telling them the whole way about the girl in the parking lot and about Rita and me, how weird we had been. "We aren't weird now," I told them. "But we were weird. Once. In olden days."

CLEO

The day before Gretchen goes to visit her family in Albuquerque, we drive over to pick up an old friend of hers, a woman named Cleo Haas. We're going shopping. Cleo has just returned from two years in California, and Gretchen is saying how happy she is that Cleo's back. "I'm talking about friends," she says. "We need to try stuff. We don't want to die in this thing."

"What thing?" I say.

"This," she says, waving her hand between the two of us. "Everything. I'm serious. I'm glad she's back. We need her. You can't just go around losing people all the time."

"We didn't move to California," I say.

"That doesn't matter," Gretchen says.

Gretchen and I have been together three years. We met in a nursery, on a Saturday. Six weeks later she moved in, bringing Cleo with her. Cleo stayed for a year, sleeping on a cot in the dining area of the apartment. Near the end of that first year we were together, Gretchen left and moved to Seattle. Cleo stayed with me in the apartment. Gretchen was gone less than a month. Early one morning she called and said she was coming back. I said that was great. Then, when she got back, Cleo left.

Now the three of us go through a department store at the mall, then split up and agree to meet at the fountain. I head for the mock outdoor café and get in line to order a chocolate-filled croissant, but a young guy with ratty hair and a silver shirt open to the waist comes in singing a torch song and pushes in front of me. He jokes with one of the girls behind the counter. They're in French-maid uniforms. I figure he's a local celebrity, maybe a drummer in some important band. The girl he's talking to likes him, which I think is amazing. I'm wondering about that when Cleo comes up.

"I hate to shop," she says. She orders a spinach croissant, then leads the way to a wire-topped table out in the mall.

I start to say something about not wanting Gretchen to go to Albuquerque, but Cleo interrupts.

"I don't do girl advice anymore. That's the way I am now. You'd better learn to work around it."

"Yes, ma'am," I say.

Cleo came back to open an aerobics franchise called Thigh High. She wears a lot of exercise gear. Today she's got on a peach-and-gray leotard under an open white shirt, a pair of baggy pants, and a yellow sweatshirt tied by the arms around the waist. Red shoes. She's good-looking—long legs, small breasts, radiant skin. Gretchen says she hasn't had a decent boyfriend since she was nineteen.

I tear my croissant in half and break off a small piece

with chocolate in it. "So, how's the new-woman business?" I ask, nipping at the chocolate.

"It's all new," Cleo says. "You ought to try it."

A girl of about eighteen comes out of a candle store, leading two children. The kids have fur animals—a red bird and a hippo. They're playing. One kid drops the bird and kicks it six or eight feet in front of her, then the other does the same with the hippo. The mother scolds them, but it doesn't have any effect.

"So, did everybody miss me?" Cleo says. She's waving her croissant around in her hand, not eating it.

"Sure," I say. "We kept bumping into something imaginary in the dining room."

"That's funny," Cleo says. "I was thinking about when Gretchen went to Washington State, you know? You were all over me. You couldn't get enough. Then she shows up and suddenly I'm bad meat. I hated your guts for that, I really did."

"I guess it wasn't my best moment. But it wasn't yours, either—you didn't want to sleep with me."

"Big deal. What is that, a way to measure something? I was a loyal guy." She playfully shoots me the finger, then shakes it for emphasis. "Never forgive, never forget," she says, finally taking a bite of the croissant.

"Don't be mean," I say.

She looks at the skylights. "This time, this time I show you what you missed. Is that nice enough?"

"That's nice," I say. "Did you see this guy inside here?" I point out the kid in the silver shirt as he leaves the serving counter. "What's the deal on him?"

"He works at Slime Land," Cleo says. "I don't know. How am I supposed to know?"

The young mother is disciplining her kids for kicking

toys in the mall. She's right alongside us now. She's bent in half and she has the girl by the wrist, whipping her back and forth, shouting in a stage whisper. The girl is crying, trying to get her fists into her eyes, but the mother is jerking her around so much the fists don't seat. "Do you want to be popped?" the mother says. "I can pop you, if that's what you want."

"Probably not what she wants," I say to Cleo.

"Hush," she says, leaning across the table.

"Hell, I think I'll go over there and give her a poke or two myself—what do you think about that?"

"Pick on somebody your own size," Cleo says, tapping her collarbone with a knuckle.

Gretchen wants to go back to Sears after we drop Cleo at her aerobics place, where some workmen are finishing the interior. I don't mind going, but I say, "Why didn't we go when we were there?"

Gretchen says, "I can go in by myself, if it's too much for you. It'll take a minute. You can sit in the car."

It's been raining all day. I take a corner too fast, bump into a curb, then bounce up on the median and rip up a bush. Trying to get out in a hurry, I mash the gas and spin the wheels, so we're kind of lurching down the street, half on and half off the road divider.

Gretchen braces herself against the dash. "This is great. Would you stop and let me drive? Christ."

"Take it easy. I've almost got it." I slow down and let a Jeep with a gray-haired woman in it go by, then I roll off the curb and into a lane. "I'm on track, headed for Sears," I say.

At the mall, I let her out, then park by the curb with the engine running for the air conditioning, then push in a tape. It's some wet-sounding rock and roll. It fits with the rain and cool-gray sky, and I sit there listening and feeling pretty wistful.

After a while Gretchen comes out of Sears empty-handed, followed by a woman in a short, red-dotted jumpsuit, and a boy who looks like her son, a thin ten-year-old. When Gretchen gets in the car, she folds her hands in her lap and stares out the windshield. "They didn't have any popcorn," she says.

"We came all the way back here for popcorn?"

"So? I like it. It's bright yellow. They soak it in butter. It's good."

"Uh-huh," I say, nodding. "You want to go someplace else for popcorn? Maybe—"

"Forget it," she says. "Let's go." She makes a shoveling gesture with her hands and rocks in her seat to illustrate going. Then she hits the direction-reverse button on the tape deck. "I hate this," she says. "What's on the other side?"

"Jason and the Scorchers," I say, but she's already hit the eject button.

"I hate them," she says. "Who are they anyway? Oh, yeah. The semirockabilly revival. I remember." She yanks the tape out and tosses it in back. "Let's just leave it alone, O.K.? Let's just go."

The jumpsuit woman is eating candy out of a small Sears bag, and the boy is slinking along beside her, one hand on her hip. They stop together on the curb, watching the drizzle. It looks as if that's the rule: whenever they're out together he has to have the hand on her hip. She holds a piece of candy for him, and he takes it with his teeth.

"She's pretty," I say, pointing to the woman. She

shakes out a clear-plastic rain hat, then curls it over her head, wraps an arm around the kid, and steps into the parking lot. The boy nestles against her, his face pressed into the curve of her waist, and they crab-walk, like a creature with two extra legs, toward a Buick parked in a handicapped zone.

"She's in love with him," Gretchen says. "If that woman ever was in love with someone else, it's over now."

"Leave her alone."

The woman unlocks the front door in the passenger's side. The boy stands off at arm's length, as if waiting for her to reach in and unlock the back door. When she sees what he's doing she leans over and gives him a hug, then steers him into the front seat.

Gretchen says, "My brother says a man doesn't really start to care about a woman until he takes possession."

"Well," I say, whining a little, rocking my head left and right. "Maybe he starts—"

She turns around, chin in hand, and gives me her drollest expression.

I say, "I think your brother's a tough guy."

"Women are the same. Look at this." She points to the kid and his mother. "He's a little monkey-boy and she loves it."

"It's good for him," I say.

"No, it's terrible. It's the same mistake. I don't want to discuss it. Can we go?"

"Sure." I get the car moving and head out of the parking lot. "Maybe I should, like, go with you on this trip. You seem to be upset."

"I thought you were the one," she says.

"I am. I just thought I might go."

"Don't be silly," she says. "Stay here. Do whatever you

want. No restrictions, reports—get something going. What about Cleo? You guys have been ripe for years."

"This morning she said she'd show me what I missed last time you left," I say. "When you went West."

"I'll tell you," Gretchen says. "Gorgeous stomach, real white skin, legs shorter than they look. Otherwise, it's a kill."

The evening is uncomfortable. I can't remember the last time there was so much distance between us. I don't know why I'm upset, and I don't know what's bothering her. She watches a show about transsexuals on TV, and I wander around the apartment, making up things to do. Now and then, I look at the screen a minute and guess whether the person talking is a man or a woman.

At eleven, she starts packing. I sit with her on the bed, watching. Finally I say, "I don't want to stay here alone."

She smiles at me.

"I'm serious. I don't want you to do this."

"Take it easy," Gretchen says. "Why don't you watch David Letterman? You like him, don't you?"

"I don't like him very much right this minute," I say.

"I don't think I like him ever," she says.

"Me, too," I say. "Now that I think about it. I used to like him."

"He's all right," she says. She's going in and out of the closet, getting clothes. "Why don't we put on some music?"

I stop looking at her, stop watching her fold the clothes and press them into the open suitcase. I roll onto my back and stare at a spot on the ceiling where the air-conditioning register has stained the Sheetrock. Then I stare at the red second hand on the clock on her bedside table. I watch it make two full circles.

"What if I have a heart attack?" I say.

"I'll find you when I get back," she says. "There'll be an investigaton. What will you be wearing?" She stops packing a minute and looks at me. "I don't know what's wrong with you. It's not the end of the world—I'm just going to see my family. It's not a big deal."

My shoulders hurt. The bedroom looks like a halfway house for magazine chic—dusty and almost correct. I feel light-headed. I say, "I'm going to end up spending the whole time with Cleo, like before."

"If that's what you want," she says. "Don't tell me about it, though, O.K.?"

"I'm telling you everything," I say.

She gives me an impatient smile. "If that's what you want," she says, finishing the suitcase.

"What about money? What are you doing for that? Are we spending my money for this trip?"

Gretchen sighs. "No, we are not. The checkbook is yours and yours alone. In perpetuity."

"Sorry. That was stupid." I get up and go into the bathroom. "Take the money, O.K.?" Before she can say anything, I twist the handle on the hot-water tap. Water splashes all over the place. I forgot about the hot water. It spatters if you open the tap too far. By the time I get the faucet off, my clothes are soaked. I go back into the bedroom, unbuttoning my shirt. "I love you," I say, stepping over her suitcase to get into the closet.

She looks at my chest and says, "Me, too."

•

The morning is no better. We talk about the plants, and how much water they need, and how much sun they need, and we talk about running the dishwasher, and about the lint filter in the clothes dryer, and that I have to remember to get the slides at the camera place, because she wants them sent to her by overnight mail. Then she has some last-minute errands to run, so she goes off to do that, and I stay at home. She gets back around noon and starts to repack her bag, but then gives that up. At three she's ready and walking around with her coffee, waiting for the cab to take her to the airport. I sit on the couch, staring at the fireplace. When the driver honks, I carry her bags, kiss her, watch her drive away, then stand on the curb, looking around at our neighborhood. The sky is overcast. The parking lots are empty.

A guy in a red truck pulls up and asks if I know where Cheryl Harrison lives. He's hanging out the window of his truck with his chin on his arm.

I tell him I don't know Cheryl Harrison.

"Crap," he says. He pops the steering wheel with the butt of his fist. "Last night I see this chick at the grocery store. You know, the one up here on Pine Tree? So I run my cart into hers and we get to talking. It seems like we're made for each other—you know that feeling? So, finally, she tells me why don't I come for a beer this afternoon, because that's when her boyfriend leaves for work and everything. I mean, she says she doesn't like to do that kind of thing, but they're having rough times and she thinks she's leaving anyway."

I shrug at him, starting to back away toward my apartment.

"She gives me this apartment number," he says. "So

I'm cool, and I write it on my arm, just like in the movies. What do you think happens?" He sticks his forearm out the window for me to see. There's some ink there, but it's unreadable.

I do a gasping sound, then say, "That's terrible."

"What it is," he says, "is I read this article about frozen Japanese dinners. You know? So, of course, I had to run out and get some." He shuts his eyes and gives his head a tiny shake. "Last night. I had to have them last night."

I'm about ten feet away from him by now. "I wish I could help," I say. "Why not look her up in the book?" Then I realize that's an invitation, so I say, "I'd let you look in mine, only we lost it in the move. We just moved here."

"Doesn't matter," he says, sitting up behind the wheel. "She isn't in the book. Or, if she is, she's in the guy's name." He shifts the truck into gear and eases it forward. "I must be getting old. I gotta stop." Then he brakes hard and the truck jerks to a halt. "You know what else? I ate one of those dinners, you know? That I bought?" He pauses for emphasis. "Lost it," he says.

I watch him drive off, then go in and freshen Gretchen's coffee and take it into the bedroom. I set the cup on the bedside table, sit on the edge of the bed, pull the curtains, look out at the path between our apartment block and the next one. On the TV screen in the bedroom there's a reflection of me with a quadrant of blue sky out the window behind. The hum of an air conditioner comes through the walls, sounding internal and basic to life. A couple of birds chirp. I hear bell-like wind chimes repeat a song pattern and wonder how the wind can do the same thing over and over. Then I hear a car horn, then a motorcycle accelerating. There's a pair of ski sunglasses on top of the television set, with the thin black elastic that runs around the neck looped down over the screen.

Some neighbors are walking the path, just below the window. The woman's voice is quick, up and down, and the man's is short, slow-sounding—a grunt. The phone rings.

"So, what's the story?" Cleo says. "She go?"

"Yep."

"How do you feel? You all right? You ready for me?"

I put a finger in the coffee to see how warm it is. "I don't know. Maybe."

"Half an hour," she says. "After that, I go for other responsibilities and obligations. You call me, O.K.?"

"How about five? I'll call at five."

"Don't push me around," she says.

"Right," I say.

"I'm ready to roll. I've been after it since first light, working the equipment. Looks terrific. You're one lucky fella."

"I know that I am," I say. "What if Gretchen changes her mind at the airport?"

Cleo does a big, exasperated sigh. "She's not changing her mind. C'mon. Two weeks is the deal. In two weeks she's back and everything's like it was. I'll be there at five. You want to go to the beach after? I can get us a place."

"Cleo," I say.

"O.K., O.K. So long."

She hangs up, leaving me with a dead line. I shake my head at the receiver, then put it away.

We go to a movie, then to dinner at a seafood restaurant on South Main, where I order fried shrimp and Cleo has king crab. It's a place with white tablecloths, heavy silverware, old paneling, waiters in faded red jackets, with huge fish on the walls.

When the food comes it looks great. I ask for some extra lemon, and the waiter zips off to get it.

"I like this place," Cleo says.

"It's good," I say.

"I was in love with you," she says. "You know? Last time." She pinches a claw, digging the white meat out with the tiny two-pronged fork. "I thought I was going to die." She dips the meat in a metal cup of liquid butter, then presses it against the rim.

"Me, too," I say.

She looks at me, making a face.

"I mean I was in love with you, too," I say.

She smiles, shaking her head. "I had fun in California," she says. "Pretty much fun, anyway. I'm a lot different now, though. I don't know if I'll ever be the same as I was."

"That's the way it happens," I say, nodding and thinking about how pretty she is.

"I'm not backing anybody up anymore," she says.

"Why should you?" I say.

"I'm picking my openings," she says.

"Right," I say. "Just like the rest of us."

She does a little take, then says, "I'm going through with this. You know that, don't you? This is the break. I do it. Bang." She narrows her eyes at me. There's a smile in them, but it's not easy.

Cleo loosens up then. We finish dinner, and afterward she drives back to the apartment, staring straight ahead the whole time. When she pulls up in the parking space, she says, "Here we are."

"So, how about some coffee?" I say.

She makes coffee, and I sit on the couch in front of the TV, switching the channels. She must know where everything is—she doesn't ask me anything. When the coffee's ready, she sits down for a minute, then takes her cup and heads into the bedroom. I watch her back, then watch the bathroom light come on, throwing a bright trapezoid on the bedroom wall. The light squeezes down to a sliver when she shuts the bathroom door.

I turn off the TV, dump my coffee in the kitchen sink, check the front door, then sit on the couch again. Water is running in the bath. It's almost twelve. For a second I think it smells funny in the apartment, but then can't smell what I thought I smelled. The light flashes across the bedroom wall again and Cleo's shadow passes through it, but she doesn't come out. She's in the closet. Then the bathroom light closes down again, only this time not as far. There's a two-foot strip of light left. The water stops in the bath.

The telephone rings. I answer it, hoping it's Gretchen. She says, "How are you?"

There's a little cracking sound on the line. I say, "I'm O.K.," then listen to the sound. "What's that?"

"What?" she says.

"That noise. You hear that?"

"I don't hear it," she says. "So—I'm at the Dallas airport. We missed the connection. I'm here for another hour at least."

"Cleo's in the bathtub," I say.

There's a pause on Gretchen's end. Then she says, "So, was I right?"

It takes a minute to figure out what she's talking about. Then I say, "I haven't looked."

"Just like old times," she says. "You O.K.?"

"I guess. We had dinner at Goldsmith's. I'd be better if you were here to protect me."

Gretchen laughs, then tells me she's going to need her recipe for lemon cheesecake, and that I'm going to have to find it in her blue recipe book. "You're going to hate me, because it's a mess. I mean, I'm going to organize it when I get back. I promise."

I take the phone in the kitchen and open the refrigerator. I stand there looking for a minute, then lift the window blinds and stare out at the cars, all the time listening to a story about a woman she met on the plane.

I interrupt her. "So what do I do?" I say, taking a bottle of spring water out of the refrigerator.

Gretchen says, "Rock her socks. It's O.K."

"You're a help." I unscrew the cap and take a drink. It doesn't taste like anything special.

She says she has to get a hamburger and a magazine, so she wants to get off the phone. I put the bottle back and tell her I love her, then kick the refrigerator closed, hang up the phone, and go through the living room to the bedroom. It's dark in there. I look at the bathroom door for a minute, then sit on the edge of the bed, just out of the light, and watch Cleo wash.

TRICK SCENERY

You have a face like an old sack, like an old vegetable, and the scenery rolls along beside you—it might be some kind of film gimmick, you don't know. You're alone and the sky is colorless, the trees shallow and black-looking. You've got an old Chevrolet, thirty-eight, thirty-nine, a convertible, a roadster, steel gray and it doesn't shine at all. You're an older man, maybe forty, and you wear your hat cocked back on your head the way reporters always do in newspaper movies, and you want a woman. You're driving a long drive, lasting several hours at least, along unused highway through unspectacular countryside—dry, dark, in some way a burlesque of menacing countryside, the way it rolls by you as if painted on a movie flat. You're tired and you want a woman, because a woman would make all the difference in the world.

Even without sun the heat of the afternoon, of the early evening, is unbearable, aggravating. With a woman the trees would be pretty and black, silky against the neutral sky—a woman has the power to change things. But you are afraid that you will never have a woman to ride with you, to wear a cheap dress from a department store and sit with you in the old roadster for the long drive along the unused highway. Resigned is perhaps a better word. And not all women are pretty, not all women will wear dresses from department stores, and it is true that some pretty women do not look so good in cheap dresses, shirtwaists, nylons and rayons, polyesters, prints and patterns with colorful belts in string loops, daring bright solids—these make some women look like they wish they were other women.

You wear a black suit with pinstripes, perhaps chalk-stripes, and a crumpled snap-brim hat pushed back on your head. You wear a vest with the last button open over your belt buckle. Your suit would be perfect for a man with a blond woman, a tall woman, her hair short and severe and only caressed by the wind (she would adjust the wing window on the front door of the roadster so that the wind would fly around her).

You see a film on television at the motel, get a late start because you wait for the film, then watch it from beginning to end sitting with your legs crossed on the unmade double bed in your room. The film is *The Tin Star* with Henry Fonda an aging bounty hunter rich in the lore of the West and of justice. You sit in your room without a woman and watch the movie on the fuzzy Motorola which the night manager says is the best set in the motel, and it isn't a wonderful film, but for you, for this moment, perfect.

You have to ask yourself why you do not have a woman. You are not a salesman. You are not a criminal or a businessman of any kind, you are a man on vacation, on a trip, with no particular destination but a strict time-table, a schedule for your return. And no woman, no bare arms to run fingers over in a festival of gesture and affection, no gently curved breasts to admire at midnight against the false brocade of a motel wall. The question is terrifying.

The radio in the Chevrolet is broken; you cannot sing.

It would be worse if you had a woman asleep in the car, a woman with sealed eyes and crooked neck, slumped beside you in the seat, her head twisted back and limp on your shoulder. A woman whose mouth in sleep became an ugly hole laced at its edges with blown hair, strands of which stuck and darkened in the beads of perspiration above the lip, stuck in the waxy gloss bordering the mouth.

So with your hat back and a curl of dark hair falling flat on your forehead above dulled blue eyes you drive, and the highway seems more endless than ever.

There is the sound of the motor of the Chevrolet, and the sound of the wind hitting the metal, and the sound of the thick rubber on the tar-filled road—these sounds dying in the night. The splash of your headlights on the road illuminates nothing.

The vacation is torment, pure and drab, but you drive and watch the wall of the landscape pass, and your three-piece suit is so beautiful. You wonder if you could not awaken the woman, wipe her face, offer her the red ball for her mouth.

PUPIL

Each summer I teach a course in BASIC at the junior college. This year Tracy Whitten is my favorite student. She's eighteen—bright, handsome, cheerful all the time. I like her braces. She's self-conscious about them, always remembering a minute too late to keep her lips tightly closed. She comes to class in shorts and a T-shirt, perspiration glinting at her temples, and we talk, and her eyes dart around as if we ought to be more discreet.

By the fourth week of the session I'm so taken with her I'm ready to break the rules. In the hall after class I say, "Maybe you could come for dinner? I'll ask some other people. We can cook out."

"Oh, sure," she says, giving me a look that means maybe I'd better think again. "That'd be real suave."

We walk down the corridor without talking, then go outside and stop near the bike rack. "I'm sorry I mentioned it," I say, making a show of looking for my car in the parking lot. "Well, not really sorry."

She smiles, wires glittering, then turns away and looks out over the baseball practice field. Today she's wearing pale pink running shorts, the shiny kind, and a thin Jack-in-the-Box T-shirt, and she's tapping her key on the rack, so there's a pinging sound in the air.

Finally, she turns around and gives me a squinty look. "I wouldn't mind coming, if you're serious."

"I am serious." That sounds too serious, so I try for a Chevy Chase joke with some stupid faces, wondering how I could have been silly enough to start this.

"Take it easy, will you? Calm down. Let me think." She watches me and does some faces that look good on her. "We know it's not a great idea. We both know that, right? It's destructive and impossible, and you're too old, and it's bad P.R."

"My speciality," I say.

She studies me for a second, then she's all smiles—patting my arm, straightening her hair, ready to walk away. "I like it. I'll come. We'll have a good time. Where is it?"

I have two bedrooms, a large living room with lots of glass, and a small garden—a side-by-side duplex, one of a hundred and ten similar units in a development that has four pools and no cleverly winding paths. I'm used to it. No so much that it feels like home but enough so that I can overlook, most of the time, the utilitarian way of things. Sometimes I even think it's pretty.

Saturday I go out and buy a barbecue cooker and the tools that go with it—tongs, a giant fork, hot-pad gloves that look like alligators. For dinner I decide to go with chicken, so I spend some time at the A&P figuring out chicken. By late afternoon I'm set up on the deck at my apartment, watching the cooker and waiting for Tracy. There's a lot of smoke around, because I've used too many mesquite chips.

I've only been out a few minutes when the doorbell rings. I go through the house to answer it, and Tracy's there with a guy about forty who has a clean face and pink skin. He's wearing black jeans.

"Hi," she says, moving her hand in a robotlike way between me and her friend. "This is George, and this is Ray. Ray's my brother, but he's really more like a pal, aren't you, Ray?"

"Sure am," he says, and we shake hands. Ray's got a soft, smooth hand and a puttylike grip.

Tracy's hair looks as if it's still wet from washing. She's got on baggy linen pants and a yellow Hawaiian shirt. She comes in first, almost bouncing, and Ray follows, giving my apartment the once-over.

I go into the kitchen to get them drinks—beer for Ray, Tab for Tracy, glasses for both of them—and I cut my finger on the pop top of the Tab can, so I have to excuse myself while I go get a Band-Aid. When I return they're already out on the deck. Ray waves at the yard. "Pretty," he says.

I look at the yard, which is small and brown.

He says, "I didn't know there was so much socializing—you know, teachers and students—out at the college."

"Sure," says Tracy. "All the time."

"There isn't much," I say. "It's frowned on."

"Yeah," he says, nodding. "That's what I thought. I saw this thing on TV about some trouble they've been having out in California. Arrests, you know . . ." He gives Tracy a glance that she, bless her heart, refuses to share. She's smiling, taking in the scenery.

"I like this," she says. "This is a nice apartment." She wipes the bottom of her Tab can down the thigh of her pants.

My neighbors are in the yard working on their bulb garden. They're a young couple with a new baby, and they have a dime-store coat of arms—a painted wood shield with "THE HERNDONS" across the top, "ESTAB-LISHED 1977" across the bottom, and a duck in the mid-dle—displayed next to their front door.

"Not much privacy," Tracy says, motioning toward the couple. "What are they doing there, anyway? Looks like they're burying something."

"Bulbs," I say.

They've been working on the garden since midwinter. It's a mound, like a grave—a dog's, or a child's. They roughed up the ground and then dumped a foot of bag dirt on top. That's where they put the bulbs. None of them ever showed up.

Ray says, "Listen, we don't need to be real nervous about me coming over here. It's just a formality. She's a full-grown woman. You're both grown. That's my feel-ing."

"Oh, Raymond," Tracy says. She turns to me. "Ray's worried about me growing up and all that. He feels bad about it." She looks at her watch, a heavy gold Timex. "How long have these chickens been on here?"

"Well," he says. "You're my sister."

The chickens are reddish brown. I'm ready for Tracy and Ray to leave, to call the whole thing off, so I stare at the chickens and say, "I'm probably out of line." I look at him, asking for some understanding. "I slipped up, O.K.? Maybe we ought to—"

"Hey!" Ray says. "Hold on. Don't get me wrong. I don't mind. She's a girl, you're a boy—you look O.K. Hell, you look like a million to me." He does a broad smile and pats my forearm.

Tracy shakes her head. "Oh, jeez. Raymond? I mean, we're not at home, O.K.?"

Ray shrugs, waving his hands around. "No more king of the dorks, huh? Well, I can't go anywhere. Helene's picking me up."

"Helene's about twelve," Tracy says.

She wraps her arms around his neck, and he pretends he doesn't like it, picking them off. "How can a person function with you all over him?"

"You wish." She grins and pushes off. "Ray's always ready to do some pretty powerful functioning."

Ray blushes, says, "That's your idea, you and Billy Hunter. He tells everybody he's helping out his secretary, and then he helps her a lot in his office."

"Billy," Tracy says, explaining to me. "One of Ray's close, close friends. He's a happening guy. I hope he catches his rear on a linoleum knife." She rattles the ice in her glass. "Anybody want soda?"

She goes in, leaving us staring at the cooker. "She's touchy," Ray says. He looks over his shoulder, trying to see into the house. "But at least she doesn't think as soon as anything bad happens it's because men run things. I told her it's ideas—all you have to do is have the good ideas. Right?"

"It helps," I say.

"Sure it does," he says. "I mean, if it ain't great, who cares who's running it?"

"Right," I say.

"Take you, for example. You've got something going. I mean, she's pretty, she's young—all that time in front of her, all this stuff to learn. Listen, I understand you college boys. You got women out there in K mart underpants, guys belong in the zoo—you can't make much of that. I mean—" He waits a second, thinking about it, scratching the back of his head. "I mean, if you're going to have a romance it ought to at least be lovely."

He thinks some more, smoothing his hair where it's standing up from the scratching. "This deal's sweet. It's a little bit stupid, but it's sweet."

I take off the cooker top and wave it back and forth trying to clear the smoke. Flames jump up under the chickens.

"Know what I'm saying?" he says.

I nod at him, then turn back to the cooker. "I'm doing these by the book, the 'indirect' method. Every time I open it I get all this fire."

"So close it," he says, taking a look at the chickens, which are getting black and crusty. "You better get those suckers off before they turn to dirt." He reaches out to wiggle one of the drumsticks and it comes off in his hand. "If I were you I'd submerge 'em for half an hour."

Tracy sticks her head out the door. "Ray? Your wealthy friend is here. This car goes by about three times, checking out the place. You want me to get her?"

"Why don't you work the chickens," Ray says. "George can get her."

Outside, the sky is thunder gray except in the west, where there's a ribbon of coral at the horizon. There's a fresh breeze, and the street lamps are on, and there's a dampness about the way everything looks. Helene is easy to spot. She's in a brilliant red 318i about half a block down from the apartment. I signal to her and, when she pulls up, introduce myself.

"Ray's inside," I say. "He asked me to come get you."

She's in her twenties, wearing a sleeveless knit cotton top and white shorts, and her arms are tan, muscular. I notice a blue vein that runs over her biceps and down her inner arm. It's prominent, easy to see.

"You must be kidding," she says. "Where's his truck?"

"What truck? He has a truck?"

"Sure does," she says. "A purple eighteen-wheeler. Lots of yellow lights."

I'm standing in the street alongside her car, scanning the parking lots as she describes these lights.

"They're great at night," she says. "He's always leaving the truck going, and you can hear it, even inside, and you look out and all the lights are sparkling—you've got to see it."

I look up and down the road. Nobody's out, but there are cars jammed up behind other cars in the head-in parking spaces. Everybody's having company. I stretch out my arms and say, "I don't know, but Ray *is* inside, with his sister Tracy."

"How do I know you're not woofing me? Maybe you're the kind of a skunk-guy who'd do a thing like that." She gives me a look as if she's sizing me up. "Naw, I guess not. Let me park this job."

I back away and wait for her to pull the car into a slot. She gets out and walks the curb as if it were a tightrope, coming toward me. "We were at the Tubes last night, me and Ray," she says, watching her feet. "You ever been there?" She shakes her head and does a little snort of distaste. "One of the great places. Really."

Out of the car, Helene's a tiny girl, easily under five feet, shaped like a bodybuilder. She says, "Ray's kind of a polecat. I don't meet many men that aren't, know what I mean? All of you got some polecat in you." She smiles at me as if she's pleased about that, then looks up ahead of us. "You live in here?"

"Yes, ma'am," I say.

She flips open the purse she's carrying and pulls out a business card, which she hands to me, holding it between the tips of her first two fingers. "This is me," she says.

The card says "SMALL PLEASURES," in chiseled-looking type, and underneath there's a printed signature— "Helene," in red—and a telephone number. I read the card, then hold it close to look at the signature. "This looks real," I say. "The signature part, I mean."

She reaches out and pats my hip. "It's a store, boyo. My own private store. Things for women." She smiles playfully. "Well, so maybe it's not only a store."

I do a little wave with the card as we go up the steps to my apartment.

"I almost called it No Man's Land," she says over her shoulder. She pops the door and it opens, and she turns around and grins at me. "But we gotta be careful."

Tracy has the chickens on top of the stove. "So what do we do with these?" she says as we come in.

"Eat 'em," Ray says. He grabs Helene and lifts her up, high, in the air, then puts her down by the window in the living room. "Hey!" he says, pointing out the window.

"A possum just went by out here. Hey! Did anybody see it?"

The dinner is quiet and quick. Helene has to have the single-volume *Columbia Encyclopedia* to sit on so she can reach the table. Tracy finishes first and moves to the brown recliner across the room, staring at the TV. Ray's watching Helene and, at the same time, talking about a hot-rod Chevrolet he persuaded his father to buy in 1957. He raced this car a lot, made his high school reputation with it.

"This one kid used to call me Rhinestone Ray," he says. "His mother bought him a Thunderbird. He hated my guts and figured this was his chance, so one night we went out and he did a triple flip into an A&W Root Beer place and I ended up going sideways across a four-lane highway, staring at headlights. Nobody was killed, but he lost a hand in the windshield. I went to see him in the hospital a couple of days later."

"This happened twenty-five years ago," Helene says. "Just to put things into perspective."

"He said he thought maybe I'd jumped the flag," Ray says, softly thumping the table with his forearm. He waits a minute, then says, "I don't know why they bought that Chevy. I mean, it was *fast*."

Ray fidgets with his glass, then turns to look over his shoulder at Tracy. "What're you up to? You're either out the door like a shot or you're sitting around staring at things."

"I'm rolfing my feet," she says. "I figure it's time to rediscover the seventies."

"Didn't we do that already?" He lifts his glass and wags it at her. "Hand me some ice, O.K.?"

Tracy gives him a look that means she'll do it but he's a jerk for asking, then comes to get the glass. He watches her go into the kitchen.

"Short legs," he says. "No way around it. Give her another couple of inches and her whole life'd be different. The teeth you fix, but you file the legs."

"You're cute," Tracy says from behind the open freezer-compartment door. She looks at me and says, "He gets this way after dinner."

"I can testify to that," Helene says.

I nod, as if I know it too.

Ray is drawing circles on the wood-veneer tabletop. "Two nights ago, I take Tracy to dinner at this steak place we always go to, and we're sitting there and this guy I knew ten years ago, a guy named Stewart, slips up behind her and starts mouthing her neck. I'm not kidding—the guy's making a mess. You figure she's going to jump or something, right? Not this one. She leans into it."

Tracy is in the kitchen doorway, listening. She's got Ray's ice ready. "I liked him," she says.

"He's greasy," Ray says. "But it's *Miami Vice* grease so it's O.K."

"Ray's afraid of *Miami Vice*," Tracy says, slipping his glass in front of him. "He says it devalues light, whatever that means."

Ray pours beer into the glass. "It means the guys are anchovies, the pictures, the music—it's the *Anchovy Show*."

"I don't agree," Helene says. "Besides, anchovies have certain desirable aspects."

"Like what?"

"Like they're silver, and if you want to you can slice them up into little tiny pieces," she says.

"I think it's silly to be afraid of a TV show," Tracy says.

"He wants to love it," Helene says. "You like the *Blade Runner* guy, don't you, Ray? He's on there. The gum-wrapper guy?"

"Yes," Ray says. He takes a drink, then fills the glass again. "I hate being on this side of the argument. I'll learn, O.K.? But first I'm going to finish this story. Please?" He turns to me. "So this guy at the steak place likes Tracy. Guys are always poking at Tracy."

Tracy makes some can-you-stop-this gestures to Helene behind Ray's back, then retakes her seat across the room.

"Poking is central to Ray's world," Helene says.

He gives her a steady look and continues his story. "So I watch and smile at all this kissing, then I wave, trying to get their attention." He demonstrates waving. "Stewart's got the leather jacket, the peach pants. He's probably got perfume going in there—"

"Smelled good to me," Tracy says.

Ray freezes and stares at her. She does a little curtsy, then pulls her foot into her lap and studies her toes, ignoring him.

Ray turns back to the table and pulls both thumbs over his shoulders in her direction. "See?" he says. "Just like that. She shuts me down like a garage door." He points at me. "Are you listening? I'm trying to say something here."

"I'm listening," I say.

Helene sighs. "Speed it up, will you, Butch?"

He gives her an instant smile. "So I'm out there in this restaurant jerking around like I'm dodging a fly. I mean, I might as well be alone."

Helene does some whimpering like a hurt animal, and then Tracy does it, too—there's a chorus of whimpers.

Ray waves both hands, giving up.

"Thank you," he says. "I want to personally thank each and every one of you for your kindness and compassion."

"Aw," Helene says. "That's real sweet."

"It's O.K.," Tracy says to me. "The place is known for flies, fat boys—green, shiny wings and everything. They make this rattling noise when they go by you. They must go a hundred or something, hundred and twenty easy. Scale speed, I mean."

I get up and start for the kitchen. "So what happened?"

"We had dinner with him," Tracy says.

Ray puts his head down on the table. "We had dinner with him," he says. "Way to go, Tracy. Way to hit the long ball out of the park."

"Well? We did."

"Yes. I know. We heard all about his life. We know where he works, we know about his wife and his kids—we saw pictures, I swear to God."

"He's a med tech," Tracy says. "He works at the pathology lab. He sits there in a room the size of a Volvo putting stuff on slides. I didn't believe him until he showed me his badge. He has to wear a badge around, to show that he belongs there."

Helene says, "Is that it?"

Ray looks at her. "See, she doesn't care if this guy crawls on her, but it's painful for me. I mean, I don't want her learning on just anybody."

"You don't want her learning," Helene says.

"That's my pal Helene," Ray says. "Casualty of the sexual revolution."

"Hey," Helene says, "I'm the big winner."

"Yeah. You and Joan of Arc."

She gets up from the table. "O.K. Time for Mr. Ray to say good night."

Tracy comes across the room and puts an arm on Ray's shoulder, standing behind him. She leans over and whispers something, then nuzzles his neck.

He looks up, pressing his head into hers, brushing her hair with his fingers, his jaw set. He gives me a wry smile.

Helene says, "Well, I, for one, had better go out and get me some dessert before I go blind."

I say, "I've got ice cream."

"That," Ray says to me, "is terrifying." He shrugs Tracy off his back and gets out of the dining chair, comes around the table, puts a hand on my shoulder and gives me a squeeze. "A fine boy." He pats my back and follows Helene to the door.

Tracy stays on her side of the table.

"What's this *blind* business?" Ray says. "I like the concept. I like the concept very much."

"Thanks," Helene says, taking a bow. "It's nothing. I do whatever is humanly possible, and if that's not good enough, why—" She pauses midsentence, pretending to have forgotten her thought. "Why, then I just do something else."

"Right," he says, looking in my direction.

I go out with them. It's cool and stars are shining; the light from the full moon is like a veil on the neighbor's Pontiac, which is in my parking place again. Somebody goes by in a bright Ryder truck. There's a faint scent of gas in the air as Ray and Helene move across the lot toward her car. It takes them a minute to get started, then they roll off down the road, taillights burning. I watch until they make a slow left at the stop sign, then go inside.

Tracy's holding a green ceramic bowl, into which she's put the leftover chicken. She says, "We want to save this, right?"

I take the bowl and dump the chicken into the paper bag under the kitchen sink. Then I get a plastic trash bag from the closet and put the paper bag in the plastic bag. I scrape the rest of the plates into the paper bag, and put the dishes in the sink, then turn on the tap full blast and use the built-in spray nozzle to rinse the plates and glasses and the silverware. Tracy's watching me do all this. I get some paper towels and wet them, wipe the countertops and the top of the stove, then the dining table. I shake the placemats over the sink, rinse everything again, then lead her out of the kitchen, hitting the light switch as we go.

"So now we start stuff, right?" she says. She grins after she says it, reaching for one of the buttons on her shirt.

She's so beautiful. Her braces are shining. On one of her front teeth there's a tiny reflection of me and of the living room behind me. I think about touching the white down on her face. I move her hand away from the button.

ARCHITECTURE

It is dark and wet. Holly sticks the credit card in her brother's shirt pocket and takes his arm: "See? I'm still Daddy's little girl."

"Don't get ugly," Park says.

She drives, hits a curb, sends bright bubbles across the hood. He bends forward to find the wipers, then clicks them on. "I'm tired. Let's go home."

"I just got the card," she says.

"I feel sorry for him."

"It isn't his fault we're . . . fond of each other, Park."

"He thinks it is."

She taps Park's shirt where the card is: "All the better for us, my evil friend."

"Cut it out, Holly," he says, drawing a mouse with a corkscrew tail on the windshield. "He's okay."

"What's that? That a mouse? You know he still wants us to see Federman, the psychiatrist."

"Federman," Park says. "Jesus."

Holly is tall, thirty, with hair cut like a man's; she wears big hiking boots and a scarf to her knees, and surplus, *Vogue* style. She hums as she steers the brown car. At a stoplight she puts both arms on the top of the wheel and points her index fingers in opposite directions: "Which way? You want to get Dzubas?"

"Here; Thirty-ninth. The one after the white one."

The stair is beige, the handrail six colors. Raw lumber is stacked neatly on the landing. Holly knocks.

Dzubas opens the door. "All my crazy sick children," he says. "You married yet?"

"Brothers and sisters can't get married," Park says.

"Watch out," she says. "Park's feeling morose."

They go to the Holiday Inn. The rooms have a connecting door, open. Holly bounces on the bed nearest the television: "What do you guys want for dinner?"

"Chicken," Dzubas says.

Park inspects the lamp switch, which is broken. "I think I can fix this with a ballpoint."

"Are french fries really French?" Holly asks, tapping the plastic menu with blue nails while waiting for the restaurant to answer. Then, outlining the drawing of the inn with her finger: "I really like hotel architecture, I mean, I really do, really."

"Steak," Park says.

"I know, I know."

Park turns to Dzubas: "How's Louise?"

"She's going to get married again," he says. He turns the television on. "To some black guy."

"See if they have fish soup," Park says to Holly.

"What kind of fish?"

"Let's go to the pool," Dzubas says.

A person finally answers and Holly recites the order and the room number, then hangs up. "We're going to eat first, remember? And we're going to that mall on the highway to get my coat."

"Is it Thursday?"

"They're open every night now."

"You know him, Dzubas?" Park asks. "The black?"

"What black?" Holly says, changing the selector on the television.

"No. He works for the PBS station here."

"Who does?"

"Louise is getting married again," Park says. "A black guy on television."

"A lot of them are doing that now," she says.

"Getting married?"

"Working on television—see? Here's one." She points at the screen, at a black newsman.

The room service person is a woman, about forty, graying. She puts the aluminum tray on the table by the window and hands the check to Park. Park hands the check to Holly.

"That was quick," Holly says, signing.

She sits down opposite Dzubas and pulls the hubs off the plates. "Why don't we go to Virginia? You want to go, Dzubas?"

He opens the curtains. "Nope." They eat looking at the parking lot.

"I love this," Holly says.

"Sure, sure," Park says.

"We all do," Dzubas says.

•

At the store Holly buys three nylon suitcases and a man's leather blazer. On the way to the car she says, "I want some pretzels, soft ones."

Park drags a bill out of his pocket and gives it to her, and she gives it to Dzubas: "Please?"

"Pick me up at the entrance," he says, pointing to a portico at the front of the mall.

When Dzubas is gone Holly says: "This isn't any fun, is it?"

Dzubas gets in the back seat and pushes a white sack into the front. "Make you fat, Holly. Park won't love you anymore."

She digs a hand into the sack. "Where to?"

"Get some sleep?" Dzubas says.

"You give up easy, Cowboy."

"It's my art."

"You know what, Park? I think we make him nervous. I think your old friend Dzubas is afraid of us, because of you-know-what."

"Plenty for me, thanks," Dzubas says, cranking his window down.

"Ease up, Holly," Park says.

"Ease up, Holly," she says, mimicking him. "Look, there's a Dairy Queen. Is that a real Dairy Queen or a fake Dairy Queen?"

"Says 'Dairy Queen.' "

"Let's get some, want to?" She twists the wheel and parks alongside a sports car.

"Mother of God," Dzubas says.

"I want a chocolate-dipped," Park says.

On the way to the window Holly slaps her thigh and

turns back to the car. "I forgot the money," she says, kissing Park on the cheek.

She stands in line behind a man in green gym shorts and another man in a suit. Dzubas says: "This is real hard, Park."

Park cranes his neck to look at Dzubas and the skin around his eyes wrinkles. "You want to go to Virginia, Dzubas?"

"No, I mean it. She's getting scary."

"Nerves," Park says. "It's because we just started up again. Getting her married wasn't such a good idea."

Holly brings the man in the gym shorts back to the car. "Needs a ride," she says, opening the door for him. "His name's Carl. Carl, meet Park and Dzubas."

"Hi, Park. Hi, Dzubas."

They drive back to the highway and Holly says, looking into the rearview mirror, "Do you work in television, Carl?"

"No, ma'am, I don't. I'm studying to be a dentist."

At a gas station Carl goes to the bathroom and Park says: "Very funny, Holly. Very endearing."

"I like him," she says, signing the charge slip.

Carl comes back wiping a brown paper rag over his face. "Man, that place is full of pinch bugs! Whew!"

Leaning forward, Dzubas taps Park's shoulder. "I think I ought to get home, Park. What are you going to do?"

"Ask Holly."

"We're going to Virginia," Holly says. "Why don't you come with us?"

"Yeah," Carl says, pulling himself forward until he is leaning on the back of the front seat. "What have you got against Virginia?"

"It scares the hell out of me," Dzubas says. Then, to Holly: "You want to let me out here?"

"What, on the highway?"

"Aw, let him out," Carl says.

"Wait a minute," Park says, when she stops the car. "Let me talk to him for a minute."

Park and Dzubas walk to the guardrail together. Dzubas picks up a bottlecap and flips it into the hazy white light of the highway. "I can get home," he says.

"I don't know what to do," Park says.

"Why don't you go home and watch TV together, like everybody else?"

"We're not like everybody else."

"Pretend."

"What do you think we're doing?"

"Pretend better," Dzubas says.

"She feels like a freak. Sometimes I do too."

"I can't help you."

A police car goes by, its siren loud. Park walks to the car and motions for Holly to get out. When she does, Carl jumps into the front seat and drives away.

Park sits on a silver-painted pole. "Way to go, Holly."

"Me? What? You talking to me? How'd I know he'd do that, huh? You told me to get out, Park."

"She's right," Dzubas says.

They walk a little way along the road without talking. A car stops beside them and two women stare out. The car is a Dodge, blue. Dzubas gestures with his hand for them to roll the window down. They look at each other, then drive away.

"Way to go, Dzubas," Holly says.

"Walking is a favorite thing of mine," Park says.

"It's a nice night," Dzubas says.

"Way to think, Dzubas."

They walk until they see a giant Gulf sign, lit over the trees. "Let's see if they have a telephone," Dzubas says.

In the cab, Dzubas gives the driver his address, then turns to Park. "You going back to the hotel?"

"What're we going to do about the car?" Park says.

Holly rests her head on Park's shoulder and looks out the cab window at the falling quarter moon. The driver drives. The tires roll on the concrete, click on the expansion joints in the highway. She says, "I'm a mess, right? That's what you guys were talking about. 'She's very untidy,' you were saying, correct?"

"Right," Dzubas says.

"You're right, you're right," Holly says. "They'll never let me back into the church. I know. I'm sorry."

"Nice night," the driver says.

CUT GLASS

A man in a room in a hotel in a city which is strange to him, a dark room, although it is night: he stands at the window looking out at the lights of the city. He is happy to be alone, although he can imagine being unhappy for the same reason. He loves the carpet in the room, the dresser, the coat hangers, the wallpaper, the padded headboard of each double bed. He has not seen the city except from the window; he has avoided every sight pictured in the hotel's *Guide to Chicago*; he will leave knowing the city no better than when he came.

He will do what he is doing: stand naked in the darkened, rented room and look out the window in peace and quiet and in pleasure.

Now he pushes away from the glass, dials Cold on the climate control, slips into the large bed, and pulls the yellow sheet and the thick spread to a point just below his nostrils.

•

Watching the local news on television he recalls visiting the city as a young man, recalls walking past a barber shop in which a barber was fighting with a customer. The barber knocked the customer down. Remembering this makes the man want to leave Chicago. He is uneasy. He closes the curtain and returns to bed but cannot sleep, so sits up and stares at himself in the mirror mounted on the opposite wall.

A blond woman says hello to him in the hallway. Her voice is cracked and slow, her breath is sweet, and when they stand together at the window in his room he marvels at her suppleness. Having noticed the dark pleasant scent of her breath he becomes worried about his own, and the conversation that is carried on is carried on with both of their faces near the glass, their breathing apparent on the pane. When he turns, finally, to brush his lips against her forehead he does not breathe, but she restrains him there, his lips on her skin, and he is forced to exhale into her hair, which smells heavenly.

She laughs then and pulls away, moving toward the dresser to make herself a drink. He watches her back as she skirts the corner of the bed; he admires her; the dress she is wearing is stylish and light, and it moves as if caught by wind as she walks.

"I want to undress now," he says.

"I don't mind."

He starts to unbutton his shirt, wondering if she has told him the truth. When the shirt is open and out of his pants he feels strongly that she has not, that it is the wrong thing to do, that undressing will reduce the moment if not the whole experience, and he decides not to continue. She asks why he has stopped.

"I'm not used to this. Ordinarily I am alone here."

Light is coming from the bathroom door, which is slightly ajar, coming from behind the woman, and he sees that she is lovely in her own shadow.

"Do I make you nervous?"

"Anyone would," he says. Then, thinking that this answer might offend her, he adds: "Yes. You in particular."

"I am nervous too. But it's pleasant, don't you agree? I'll go if you like."

"No. Well—not yet, not yet."

She goes into the bathroom. The man switches the television off and on several times, quickly, then undresses and gets into the bed nearest the window, stretching his legs and feet toward the corners of the mattress.

"Usually I'm here alone," he shouts into the darkness, toward the bathroom.

When she is into the second bed he says, "Usually I'm alone," then feels foolish for having repeated himself and pushes his hand out in the direction of the bed she is in. It is an uncomfortable moment because when his hand first reaches her bed she does not know that it is there and he has to pat the mattress to get her attention. Then, after a time, in the darkness of that hotel room in a city with which he is by choice unfamiliar, he feels cool wetness between his fingers and feels her blond hair softly fallen on his wrist, and he realizes that she is kissing his hand with her tongue, and laughing.

In the morning at the newsstand she says: "This is as far as you go."

"Yes. But I fly a lot. All over. I have a friend to meet today, upstairs."

"A friend?"

"Not a woman."

She leaves and he buys copies of *Domus* and *Abitare* from the clerk and returns to his room, to the chair by the window. He studies the magazines carefully, taking pleasure in the lovely homes on mountainsides, in canyons, homes of very modern design, homes in which plainness is elevated to unbearable beauty.

The woman calls the hotel from her office. He has opened the window and there is the smell of spice, of cinnamon, in the room.

"I'm coming back tonight."

"Good."

"Do you know who is dead? Sartre."

"I know."

"I think it's very curious that Sartre is dead, don't you?"

"I suppose he should be. Dead, I mean."

"Exactly."

He takes a long bath and goes back to the window with a towel around his waist, a towel draped on his shoulders, and a towel over his head. There are people walking in the street and along the waterfront, brightly colored people, and the wind has shifted, and he can no longer smell the spice.

When she returns they shake hands and then she laughs and pulls him into an embrace, kisses the still wet hair behind his ears.

"Hello," she finally says.

He notices that she looks tired, that her dark skin is

rougher than he remembers, that her hair is more brown than blond and less well cut than he thought.

"You're marvelous," he says.

She turns from the window. "Thank you."

"My friend," he says, looking past her toward the Hancock silhouette against the closing sky, "my friend is not my friend anymore. He has gone crazy, I think."

She says: "Do you have a cigarette?" and he imagines that she sounds like a wonderful movie actress.

"In my jacket." He is pleased that she will leave her scent in the pocket of his coat.

She stays at the window with both hands in the waistband of her jeans.

"I want to smell your hands," he says.

Smiling, she pulls her hands out of her waistband and walks to him holding her hands out palms upward. He takes the hands in his and bends his face to them, smelling the palms, backs, wrists, each in turn, inhaling deeply, slowly, each in turn, until she moves both hands up against his eyes. She holds them there, pressed tight, and he is made acutely aware of the shape of his face, of his cheekbones and the bones over his eyes, and of her hands, slight, almost skeletal, hard.

"I like this very much," he says.

He tells the woman that he has decided to stay in Chicago, that he wants her to stay with him, at the hotel.

"Can I do that?"

"Don't pretend to be silly."

The night is deeply hazed; lights out the window are ringed with glares in which they can see small rainbows. The man and the woman sit on the two beds, talking little; he does not drink so much as he did the first night, she does not drink at all. They sit watching the mist tighten on the glass.

She brings two suitcases and a tote and fills the bathroom with her scents, her perfumes and soaps. The following day, while she is at work, he goes through her things as if they were pieces in a treasure, touching them softly, turning bottles against light, savoring, gently tracing outlines of objects with his fingers.

He is in the bathroom when she returns.

"What's going on?"

"Just a minute," he says through the locked door.

She drops her coat on the chair and her attention is drawn to the view: the day is crisp, even cold, and looking out the window she realizes that from that vantage it is not possible to tell exactly what the weather is, that it could as well be warm and overcast, or humid, or even bitterly cold, much colder than it actually is. What is most curious to her about this is that something so obvious should have gone unnoticed.

The man comes out of the bathroom with her beige dress.

"Playing with my dress?"

"I want you to wear it again." He drops the dress on the bed behind her.

Automatically unbuttoning her blouse and tugging it loose from her pants, she hands it to him as one might hand a shirt in need of ironing to a valet. "I suppose you'll want this right away."

He stretches out on her bed and drops the blouse over

his face. "It looks funny through this," he says. "You're vague-looking."

"Swell. I called at half-past three."

"Many magical things happened."

"The message lamp is still blinking."

"Let it blink all night, I like it."

"Why do you stay here? It gets on my nerves, it already gets on my nerves. It doesn't work like this, people don't do things this way."

"They would if they could."

"You can't even tell what the weather's like."

"Sure I can; it's cold. I felt the glass."

"It's not just the weather, for God's sake."

They sit in silence. He watches the goose bumps appear on her naked shoulders, then disappear, then appear again; she looks out the window at the graying sky.

When he wakes up the next morning she is packing.

"I don't understand," he says.

"You understand."

"Right, I understand. But I think you're wrong."

He sits up in bed and sniffs the air, twists his head back and forth. "The smell, the scent—is that you?"

"Who else?"

"No, I mean it's new, isn't it?"

"Yes."

"Where'd you get it? Was it here?"

"Bought it yesterday, downstairs."

"It's wonderful," he says. "Everything we need right in the building."

She kisses him softly on the cheek and he holds her, puts his arms around her.

"This is awkward," he says.

She pulls free of him and walks to the door. He looks at the window, stares at it, at its whiteness and the way it seems to push itself into the room.

"It's very pretty," he says. "To see it close like this is very pretty."

She lines her cases at the door and takes a last look at the room. It is snowing. Flat spots of white slip down and across the window. The buildings of the city are obscured by the dense snow and the glass has the look of a wall. She dials room service, then sits beside the man on the bed, and they wait, and the bellman comes, and she gives him bills, and he takes the bags away.

CHROMA

licia's taking her weekend with her boyfriend
George. It's part of our new deal—she spends
every other weekend with him, plus odd nights
in between. The rest of the time she's with me. When we
started this I thought it'd drive me crazy. One time I
actually slugged her. I was sure she was leaving me, but
as it turned out she didn't want to leave at all. She wanted
to stay. She said meeting George was fate, an accident,
that she didn't plan it. I guess I accepted that. Then I
started liking the days alone every two weeks. It's quieter,
the house is cleaner—things don't get messed up. I don't
have to schedule around her. It's as if we have joint
custody, George and I.

I'm spending Saturday with a neighbor named Juliet.
She's in her twenties, a graduate student recently sold on
health—free weights, the gym, night classes in anatomy.
She owns the house next door with her girlfriend,
Heather, who's thirty-five, tall and angular, and runs
boutiques.

Heather's on a shopping trip, which is how Juliet and I happen to be together. It's raining. We're in an old section of town—lots of storefronts turned into eight-table restaurants—looking for a place to get a late breakfast. We hustle from one to the next, deciding each is wrong on decor, grease, or eaters. Finally, we go to this fried-chicken shop on Berry Lane called Bill's. It's been there thirty years, so all the things wrong with it are deeply wrong, which seems to make it O.K. There's a lot of big, old rope in the restaurant. Besides, Juliet's been there before.

Juliet thinks I'm depressed. She tells me this and asks several times what it is that's bothering me. I make up the usual stuff, trying to avoid the question, afraid that if I start to tell her, I'll end up saying a lot of junk now that won't be true this afternoon. She gets a chicken-fried steak and I go for the chicken, and we eat watching the plastic tablecloth.

"We aren't very good friends," she says.

"Sure we are," I say. "C'mon."

"O.K.," she says. "O.K. Tell you what. When we go back to the house I want to make love to you."

I'm cutting meat off a drumstick right at this point. I've had most of the skin and now I'm looking for what's left. I say, "Oh?"

"I think it's necessary and important," she says.

I get my fork into a piece of meat and whisk it around in the gravy that has slipped out of my mashed potatoes.

"Fair's fair," she says.

That's the last I hear of it until we get home. I park in my driveway and she comes around the car and takes my hand, marching me across the grass toward her house.

All the houses around here are one-story brick jobs, paneled dens, sliding-glass doors looking out to back-yards. She puts me on the sofa, which in her place faces the sliding door and the red patio where they barbecue. I notice they don't have a Weber, it's something else, one of the flatter, squarer kinds. Maybe it's from Sears or some-thing. The trees out there are bent and dripping.

I say, "I don't know. We're friends, but we don't have to do this." I have the idea I'm taking the top line on the thing.

Juliet's moving around between me and the window, not really doing a show, but sort of doing a show. "Sex is my guts. It really makes me sting."

"Uh-huh," I say. I get off the couch.

She laughs, the muscles in her neck rippling prettily. She's got a lot of muscles. "I'm sorry. That was dumb. I was just trying to be, you know, seductive." She sud-denly droops, going limp on the couch. "So I guess we ought to forget it, huh?"

I come up behind her and rub her hair in this way that's much more awkward than I intend, then I stop that and get down behind the sofa so that our heads are about at the same level. Only our eyes are above the sofa back. I say, "It's real sweet," and put the emphasis on "real," and now I'm doing her hair in a much better way. It's work-ing. "It's a lovely idea, it's very flattering, but . . ."

"My friend Allie?" Juliet says. "She told me about this one time she made love in front of a bank in Paris at two in the morning with this girl she met on one of those boats they have? There was a French dumpster in the street there, and they got in—she said it was crazy. She said she couldn't walk right after. She says when it feels that good you know it's gotta be true."

I look at her real slow, giving her what I imagine is my older-and-wiser look.

"She married the dumpster?" Juliet does a smile that's kind of sad around the edges. "Maybe I'll just put on a record—you think that'll help?"

She does wobble-knees on her way to the stereo and plays something by Nat King Cole, and it's on tape, not record. The music gives me gooseflesh. I haven't heard Nat King Cole since the seventh grade, and I feel like crying about it. I get up and stand behind Juliet, wrap my arms around her and hold her, listening to this awful music, thinking it's crushing the way she loves, that she's such a child.

She says, "Is this O.K.?"

I say, "Sure," and let her take me back to the couch.

Juliet's nice—we hug some more, kiss a little, mostly sit and stare at the points where our bodies touch. We don't talk. I feel close to her, like I want to protect her from everything.

At four I'm out driving around in the family car, trying to figure out what kind of takeout food I want to take out for my dinner. At a stoplight somebody jiggles a rubber fish out the window of a bus next to me. It's a pale green fish, about ten inches long—shark, or whale. I've seen lots of them, beach toys. I'm a little behind the bus, in the next lane, bent over the steering wheel trying to see who's doing this fish. I think it's a kid, then realize it's Heather, and she's signaling me, so I nose in behind the bus and wait while it discharges people. Then I unsnap the door lock and move up so she can get in.

"Howdy," she says, sliding in alongside me.

"Hi," I say. I reach out and touch her hand, waiting while a carpet truck goes by, then steer into the center lane and say, "Got yourself a belt-fish."

"What's a belt-fish?" She holds the fish up in front of her and carefully looks it over.

"That," I say. "You put the tail under your belt and then walk around just like normal. A guy I know is the father of the belt-fish."

She shakes her head and drops the fish into a shopping bag. "I don't know what you're talking about. This is a present for Juliet, who is fish crazy." She crinkles the bags getting settled. "I was downtown. I used to go down there on the bus to the Majestic Theatre, where I saw *A Fistful of Dollars*, and some Bond movies, the first couple. Today I went to a mall in an office building and bought shirts. Have you looked at shirts? They're nuts. These people think we're fools."

I give her a squint. "Which people?"

"The ones with the shirts. I got four shirts and a bathrobe for three hundred eighty dollars." She reaches over her shoulder for the safety harness. "So how's the perfect Alicia?"

"O.K.," I say.

She makes a sorry-I-asked face and nods knowingly. "Oh. Her weekend. That would be . . . George?"

I point at her.

Heather doesn't believe spouses should tell each other too much. We've had this argument before. I say it's easier to handle what you know about than what you imagine, and she says it's better to keep your mouth shut and your eyes closed.

She grins. "You guys still playing Donkey Kong, huh?"

I wait a minute for that to make sense and, when it doesn't, say, "I don't know what that means, Heather."

She shrugs. "Me either. I just said it. I guess it means that it'll never work. You let this go on much longer and she's going to think you don't love her anymore."

"She knows I love her."

"Well, she may know it but not think it."

I lift an eyebrow at her and do some blinky stuff with my eyes. "Logic needs work," I say.

"It's possible," she says. "Tell you what, you and Juliet quit coveting and I'll let her deviate his septum for you—is it a deal?"

"I thought that was my secret."

"You don't believe in secrets," Heather says, flapping her hands like a pair of toe-heavy socks on a line in a wind. "But hey! You guys over there do what you want. It doesn't bother us. We can be savage. We wouldn't be *we* very long . . ."

"She wants something interesting in her life. There's no big harm in it. You can't blame her."

Heather says, "I'm not blaming her, I'm blaming you."

I swerve to miss a broken-up microwave somebody has dumped in the street. When I get going straight again I smile a patient smile.

"I don't know. Whatever works, right? This is the eighties." She makes a flustered, dismissive move with her hand. "Let's forget it. I don't even know what I'm talking about." She's doing flat karate chops in front of her. "I'm having my ongoing struggle with the language," she says.

"Ah, language," I say.

"You touch the doughnut girl, I'll do your teeth in piano wire," Heather says, grabbing her front teeth for emphasis.

Alicia is staking potted plants when we drive up. I don't know why she's home, except that sometimes, on her weekends, she comes back for a couple of hours, to get different clothes, or just to say hello. She waves with something that looks like a car antenna. Heather shakes the fish at her.

Alicia says, "Nice fish."

"We call him Morodor," Heather says.

Alicia taps Heather's arm with the antenna. "Well, who's going to get my cactus? It's by the kitchen door and it weighs three hundred pounds."

"We don't speak power lifting," Heather says.

"She got new shirts," I say. "Very expensive. I found her on the bus."

Alicia looks next door, toward Heather's driveway, at the Volvo parked there. "Something wrong with this car?"

"Nope," Heather says, spreading her purchases on the hood of our car. Alicia and I nod at each shirt. I stop Heather on a black one with a thin silver diagonal stripe, a shirt she says cost a hundred and forty dollars.

"That's mine," I say.

Heather shakes her head, slipping stuff back into bags. "If it's new it's wrong—that's my feeling. You see the pockets on these guys? I don't know. It's a big risk."

Alicia says, "They'll be great. Carry books in there."

"Books?" Heather falls back, holding packages up as if to protect her eyes from a bright light.

Alicia says, "I'm making eight-thousand-jewel rice for dinner and you're invited."

"You're here for dinner?" I say to Alicia.

"Yeah. Sure." She shoves me a couple of times. "What's it to ya?"

When Heather leaves I bring the cactus around, hurting my back in the process. I sit with Alicia while she plays with this plant, trimming parts off, giving it a bath, fertilizing it, putting sticks in the dirt trying to get it to stand up straight.

I'm on the concrete with my head dropped back against the brick window ledge. I say, "She asked about George."

Alicia thinks a minute, but doesn't speak.

I narrow my eyes at her. "That had the look of something there."

"If I thought something I only thought it for a second and I don't remember what it was, so leave me alone."

"Yes, ma'am. Moon rises when you hove into view."

She does a little bow. "Thank you. Why don't we hove on in for a nap? You can hold me. What do you say?"

I put an arm around her and pull her toward the door.

Heather and Juliet arrive at eight on the nose, Heather in jeans and a brown blouse, Juliet in chrome-yellow shorts and one of the new shirts, the black one with the diagonal stripe. It falls open at the slightest deviation from perfect posture.

Alicia brings them into the living room, where I'm fixing the feet on the coffee table. "He's into handy,"

Alicia says. "Here, he's being handy under the coffee table."

Heather does a polite smile and picks up an audio magazine off the table, easing into the couch.

"Can I turn this on?" Juliet says, stopping in front of the television. "See how the Braves are doing?"

"Sure," I say.

"Keep it low, O.K.?" Heather says. "We're guests."

Juliet says, "Gee, Mom. If you're sure Mr. Anderson won't mind."

"I'm sure," Heather says.

George calls in the middle of dinner. Alicia answers the living room phone, then moves to the bedroom and has me hang on for her. I listen to him breathe a minute, then hear the click of the other phone and Alicia says, "I've got it."

I go back to the table. Heather and Juliet are looking hard at their plates. Juliet has pushed her food out to the edges of her plate, so it looks like a wreath.

"Just eat it," Heather says to her. "Let's don't attack the poor man with food play."

"Hey," I say. "Who's poor here? I'm licking wounds as fast as she can inflict them."

Juliet gives me a look I like a lot, a sweet look out of the tops of her eyes. We stare at each other for a minute and it's like some force is shooting back and forth between us, like vases are rattling on their tables.

It makes Heather nervous. She stares at Juliet until she gets her attention. "Settle down," she finally says. "Let's don't O.D. on the compassion thing."

After they leave I watch Alicia fix up the kitchen and, when that's done, make a sandwich and sit on the cabinet eating it. I take a diet Coke out of the refrigerator and sit with her, watching her eat, telling her about Juliet. She listens, eyeing me carefully as if to see what my face might give away that I won't quite be able to say. When I finish she takes a long pause, staring at the part of the sandwich that remains. She has picked off the crust, and pinched the rest into some kind of animal shape.

"I don't like it," she says.

"What?" I say.

"All of it. Any of it. You're supposed to sit here and love me and me alone while I go out and do the rope-a-dope all over the place. Isn't that the deal?"

I look at her.

"So what's this about? I mean, we got melancholy in the mug here." She points the sandwich fragment at my face.

"Mug?" I say.

"Whatever." She downs the sandwich and slides off the cabinet, smacking her hands together. "I guess it's fine if you like tragic longing. Are you going to be O.K. if I go out?"

"I'm fine," I say.

"You look terrible. Maybe I ought to stay? You look like you're going to hang yourself, or slit your throat, or something. Call your girl."

"I'm O.K.," I say. We're standing in the middle of the kitchen and we sort of self-consciously lean toward each other, then start hugging, shy at first, then tight. It's nice to feel her against me again, how warm she is, how strong she is. We rock side to side like that for a minute, then pull apart.

I say, "Well, I guess I won't hang myself."

"Cute," she says.

I head for the bathroom. Alicia follows me and watches me brush my teeth. "I think I like her," I say, stopping in the middle of brushing, holding the toothbrush in my mouth.

"You'd like her more if she was on you like bug repellent." She gives me one of those woman looks, the kind that usually comes complete with poised eyeliner brush.

I say, "I'll take some roaches next time."

She's twisting her head back and forth to check her teeth in the mirror. "Take rats," she says.

There's a tiny double beep on a car horn from the driveway. George. He isn't allowed in the house. When he comes for Alicia he pulls up in his Porsche and taps the horn. I've never heard such a discreet beep as George's.

She says, "I feel funny about this. Why am I always leaving? Am I ever staying home anymore?"

I give her a look that means it's the wrong time and the wrong question, and then walk her to the door. I go out on the porch so George gets a good look when I kiss her. "Don't be late," I say.

I'm inside in front of the television before they have a chance to pull away. The TV sound is annoying, and then, when I cut the sound, the things on the screen seem strangely distant, like from another world. That's O.K. for a minute, but then I feel sad, so I hit the remote button and sit there on the couch, stretched out, looking around the room. Nothing's out of place. It's dark and spotless. I sit there thinking about Juliet, seeing her in disarray, twisted up on the sofa, or relaxed in her bed, or on the floor next to the exercise bike. She's incredibly lovely and sexy in my imagination. Then I think about how fast things fly through your head when you're thinking, about how you see only key parts of stuff. I look at the cover of an issue of *Artforum* that's been on the coffee table for the last two months. It's this painting of an upside-down kangaroo I like pretty much. The only light in the room is from outside, a mercury vapor street lamp that leaves the shadow of the Levolors stretched along one wall, broken by a gladiola on the pedestal where we always put outgoing mail. The shadow has a flicker to it. I get a fresh drink and sit there watching this shadow and feeling like somebody in an Obsession ad, sitting there. I put my feet up on the far arm of the couch and drape my hand over my eyes, staring at this shadow—it's gorgeous. I unbutton my shirt and pull it open. I wish Juliet were with me, on the floor, leaning against the couch, so I could touch the back of her skull, comb her hair with my fingers, watch her cigarette smoke, blue against the perfect gray of the room. I think about tracking my knuckles on her cheek, resting my hand on the freckled skin of her shoulder. I imagine our conversation cut with pauses, her voice always hanging in the dry silence of the room like something lost.

The next thing that happens is I hear the doorbell and don't know what's going on. I think it's tomorrow. I get to the kitchen and look at the clock, see it's eleven-thirty, and wonder why it's so dark at that time of morning. Then I figure out I fell asleep on the couch, and go answer the door.

It's Heather. I say, "Hi. Come in."

"You're a real pony," she says. "With Juliet. I hear she offered the full show this morning." She brushes past me into the house, hitting every light switch she can find. "How long have we been friends?"

I squint at the street. "Pony?" I shut the door and follow her into the living room. It's too bright in there. "Years," I say.

She sits in one of the straight chairs. Her clothes are stuff I've seen in magazines, but that she never wears—balloon pants that get clownish about the calf, a shirt similarly enlarged, skinny purple shoes. "I ought to use an ice pick on her gums," she says, drilling a finger back and forth under her nose.

I say, "It's O.K., Heather. We're friends. Nothing happened. It was a sweet gesture. Nobody took it seriously." I look at my hands, backs first, then palms. My neck feels thick. I sit on the forward edge of the couch and crack my knuckles.

"Juliet," she says.

"Yes," I say. "That's why it was sweet."

She watches me do four or five fingers, then starts to fidget with her hands, doing what I'm doing. "I can't do that. It's supposed to be so easy, but I can't even do it."

"Sure you can," I say. I crack my forefinger by looping my thumb over the first joint and pressing hard. "Try it."

She does what I'm doing. There are no pops, so I take her hand and try to do the knuckles myself, but I can't. I say, "No knuckles."

She pulls the hand away and stands up, heads toward the kitchen. "I don't want us in your mess. I can't handle organized infidelity."

I say, "She was being kind, Heather. C'mon. What mess are we in, anyway?"

"Sick-o," she says. "The wife's out with a college kid,

doing God knows what, and you're around hitting on the neighborhood girls. Feeling modern."

"I feel lousy," I say. "As a matter of fact."

Alicia's back before midnight. I'm listening to cassettes I've made of a tune off a solo guitar record, comparing three different kinds of chrome tape. They sound the same to me, but I keep listening, trying to find the differences. Alicia says I should come talk to her while she bathes. I finish with the tapes and shut off the recorders, giving her a minute to get settled, then go knock on the bathroom door.

"Hello?" she says.

In the bathroom I sit cross-legged on the bath mat, facing her. She's lying in the tub, hair up, eyes shut. She's having a bubble bath, but her shoulders are out of the water, wet and shining. I look at her for a long time before I say, "I didn't sleep with Juliet."

"I know," she says. She doesn't open her eyes.

"It was O.K., though. We touched a lot. I had a great time. She had a terrific time. It changed our entire lives."

"Good work," Alicia says, sitting up in her bath. Her shoulders curve forward into hollows at her collarbone. Her breasts are spotted with bubbles. She starts soaping the sponge and the bubbles sizzle.

I nod. "I was feeling mighty crazy."

"I believe that," she says.

"It wasn't too bad," I say.

I stare at her, thinking how gorgeous she is—cheekbones, the shape of her face, her eyes, the skin. I like her skin because it's rougher than most women's, kind of Texas prairie-looking, toward swarthy. I look at the tiny scar, three-sixteenths of an inch, right of center over her lip, and I remember her telling me how she got it—going over a chain-link fence to a boyfriend's at age eleven. She has three other scars on her face, all imperceptible unless you know where to look, and each with a story. A baseball bat, a fall from her father's shoulder, a car wreck.

I say, "You look great. You look high tone, like you ought to be at some bop club."

That makes her nervous. She starts messing with her hair, dropping nests of bubble bath.

I sigh. "So Heather comes over and says we're in trouble, and she doesn't want trouble like ours, and how come I have to mess with Juliet."

"I was wondering that myself," she says. She's waving the sponge back and forth between us. "Are we in trouble?"

I shrug. "I don't know. You tell me."

She cups some bubbles and looks at them up close. She pokes them with a finger on her free hand. "My guess is we don't have to be if we don't want to be," she says. She shakes her head. "I mean, we're made of steel, right? We're the ones."

"Right," I say.

"We make the rules, we write the songs."

"Right."

"Are you O.K.?"

"I'm good," I say.

She rinses her legs, then turns to me and holds up both hands as if she really wants to straighten something out. Now. In some big, final way. "Look," she says. "I don't want you to think I'm not a serious person, O.K.?" She looks at me, waiting.

"What?" I say.

She says, "I mean—could you use some cheese ball right about now? I am *dying* for cheese ball. I've been thinking about it all night long. I'll even make it."

I sit there looking at her, my chin cupped in my hand. I'm wondering about how to react to that, about how I feel about it, about her, trying to figure that out. After a while I reach out and put my hands on the edge of the tub—they're like bird feet, thumbs on my side, fingers on hers—and I pull myself up to my knees so I can kiss her.

She laughs. She's so beautiful.

ALUMINUM HOUSE

You stand by the door. Two men slide a woman on a stretcher into the open back of a dusty truck on a cheap street in Mexico City, where you have lived much of your life, and you watch the woman's fingers tighten on an old, painted comb, her face turned oddly back and up, her lips a thin violet. Adriana, your sister, says, "She's dead now," and you sigh and reply, "Stupid! Look at the hands!" But you know that Adriana is right. The truck moves—too slowly—and the old woman's flesh bounces unpleasantly. Birds swing out of the sky and toward the windscreen, then flash away. Adriana sits on a metal chair, her eyes low, the knot of her tie neatly imperfect, and draws a heart on the scummy glass, then turns the heart into a picture of blue hills, then into spectacles on a narrow-faced man. "I expected this," she says, "something like this, anyway. We'll go to the airport directly—tell the driver, hurry, we're stopping." Something catches your eye and you swivel toward the window, but at that moment a laundry van, black with a baby painted on the door, passes between you and what had caught your attention. Adriana says, "I knew this was going to happen."

You don't remember your father. In the cab the attendants pass a single brown cigarette back and forth, each puffing vigorously in turn. You tap the small window and tell the driver that the old woman is dead, that you want to go to the airport, but at that moment a fat man steps on the running board and the driver turns abruptly, gesturing toward the passengers, toward you. The fat man moves along the side of the truck and, holding his hand to the window to shunt the glare, peers inside, and the three bright rings on his fingers snap against the glass. "Doctor," he says, and thumps himself on the sternum. "She's dead," Adriana shouts back. "We're taking her to America."

The airplane is no longer shining, except a wing flap, a few panels near the hatch which have been replaced, and you sit by the woman, tucking the loose sheet, pushing and pulling the sheet, brushing dust away from the woman's completely covered face. You remember that you are nine years your sister's junior, and think that much is lost to you by that fact and accident, and that what is lost will not be recovered—a plain thought which, along with the recurrent image of a painfully pretty young man talking with attractive women in department stores, troubles you during the flight to Tampa, and the following flight to Fort Myers. Finally there is a waiting hearse and a soberly dressed man and a rented sedan for you and your sister to drive away in, and you do that, drive away to the motel and take a room on the second floor overlooking the pool which is full of children who remind you of yourself, inevitably. Adriana talks to your father's nurse on the telephone, then leaves, and you decide to take a walk. The day is cool, sticky, the air from the coast makes a thin mask on your face. The frame buildings you see remind you of buildings you've seen before, but you know they are not the same buildings. The people at the Gulf station seem familiar to you: they walk in circles around huge cars which have boats attached, and there are children in the cars, and gaily clad mothers, and men in starched green shirts. At the café there is a waitress with a bouffant and a second waitress who is quite old, and the two women sit together at a table near the window and look out at you as you walk past. The neon sign above the parking lot is off and opaque and white against the afternoon sky.

The funeral is brief and like a thousand others: at a given moment on a certain day in a particular place a woman is packed into the ground and suddenly, briefly, remembered. You know none of the mourners, and Adriana does not know them, but she speaks to each old man and woman softly, touching and being touched in an oddly objective way. Heads turn repeatedly toward the dark hole in the ground. You notice that the machinery used to lower the casket is safely out of sight beneath pads of false grass. "Let's go," Adriana says when all the mourners have gone. "His house isn't far from here, we can walk." She turns you at the edge of the cemetery and you walk in empty midmorning streets lined with bungalows, white, well-kept bungalows.

•

"I don't feel well," your sister says, and she takes a straight chair in the living room, reaching for a magazine. You follow the young nurse along a squat hallway and into your father's bedroom. He is small, frail, curled in the bed like a garden slug. His arms are immensely thin, bare, and dust white. When he spies you he pushes his queer body back into the pillows and tells you to sit. He has some things to tell you, some many things. He is an old man, older today than yesterday, older tomorrow than today. You are not to interrupt him with questions. You sit tensely on a chair close to the bed in the low-ceilinged room there in Florida and listen, for the first time in your life, to your father. He is an old and moral man, he believes in doing right even though it is hard to do right in this world and even though in this world right means many things. It is easier to learn as a child, and he learned, and he has not forgotten. He has been sick for several years, bedridden since his sixty-first birthday, the celebration of which was too much for his heart, and his skin bruises easily now and the bruises are uglier than they were once. He is cared for in his decline by a woman, young and very pretty, very womanly—your sister, Adriana. Before the stroke he could not stand her company because of the thoughts a father has and cannot avoid because a father is a man. He never saw her, never spoke to her. But now that he has accepted half of death, he has found life, now he looks at her hair, at her skin, and he takes the simple pleasures. Your father pauses and you wonder if you should correct him, point out that you and Adriana have only just arrived, that the woman who cares for him is a nurse, but you decide against telling him, and pull your chair closer to the bed, place your hands on the bit of sheet he has thrown aside.

He goes on. He should tell you something about life, about his life: he has a pan for his toilet and a second pan for his bath, it's clumsy, but with your sister's help he is comfortable—but that is not what he wants to tell you. You watch the old man struggle with the top of a tall clear bottle from which he finally manages to retrieve the inevitable pill, which he takes without water. The effort seems to drain him and he falls back into the pillows, his eyes shut and his breathing thick. You hear him say, wheezing, that he watches her breasts like a boy watches the breasts of the women who visit his mother—it's not good. He allows himself to imagine her breasts, her sweet curved belly, the lank of her young legs, he gives himself an increasing clarity and vividness in thoughts of touching her slightly, even accidentally, in those places he imagines to be so beautiful, so dark and gardenlike— your father stops talking and closes his eyes, remember- ing what he remembers, and then, as if on cue, the nurse reenters the room clutching a battered copy of Willa Cather's *My Antonia*, and she sits on the bed opposite you and takes your father's hand and begins to swing it, pivoted at his elbow, gently in a short arc above the bed.

"You're a fine young man to come to see your father all the way from South America," she says.

MAGIC CASTLE

There is a woman in the shopping mall sitting alone on a bench by a fountain painted that green reserved for fountains, next to a bewildered-looking American Indian. The mall is the new town center, several miles outside of the town but still the center as these things are measured, and it is filled with shoppers and strollers all around, shopping, strolling, eating ice-cream sticks and letting go of children, people watched by, and unaware of the small, still-young woman in the bright coveralls who has just begun a conversation with a friendly passerby. "I was telling this Indian about the magic castle, about how pretty the great walls, the green dungeons, the bold turrets thrown against the sky—a marvelous sight!" she says.

He says, "Really?"

"Saw it with mine own eyes, these eyes," she says.

"They're very pretty, those eyes. What's with the injun? He a friend of yours? He looks a mite peaked," he says.

"Sure does, don't he?" She looks at the Indian.

"And the name there on your pocket," the passerby says. "That yours too? Mary?"

"Call me Mary, Bub, if you please," she says.

"Mary, you have one hundred percent remarkable eyes," he says.

"Amen, amen, thank you, and oh, the great yacking glory of what they seen, Bub. Oh, I could tell you stories."

"Call me Bub," he says. "Listen, you live hereabouts? Work for the government?"

"Year-round right here in San Antonio, Texas, yessir. And the government too, by damn, right again—Bub, you're a wizard."

"Thank you. Now about your friend?" He points to the Indian. "What's his status?"

"Spinning Eyes, the amazing warrior chief of the Cheyenne, don't you know, spouse of the infamous Flying Object."

"No kidding? Can he talk?"

"Ha! Talk your ear off if he gets a chance. Here, I'll show you—say hello, Spinning."

"Hiya," the Indian says.

"See there? Ain't no real true friend of mine, though, I just met him. Come up here all sneaky like while I was just sitting and thinking about my sins. Says he's looking for Mister Microphone just like the rest of us, looking for the New York white woman which was once his squaw."

"That'd be before his marriage to Object," the passerby says.

"Yep. Right after Sand Creek, far as I figure."

"Sand Creek is a terrible burden on the white man," he

says. "That's for sure. I saw a movie about that very thing last night. Starred Candice Bergen—you see that one?"

"Seen 'em all, Bub. First to last. Inside out. That Eleventh Colorado was a bad bunch, sure as hormones."

"So do you think we could get Spinning Eyes to take a little walk and leave us alone to pursue our own particular interests, whatever they turn out to be, if you know what I mean?"

"Why, Bub! Sure." She turns to the Indian. "Uh, listen, pal, why don't you take a shag? Maybe see if you can't scare up some rabbit or something. What say?"

The Indian doesn't say anything.

"Give us a minute to think on it, Bub," she says. "Remember, he's not urban like you and me."

"We've got a lot in common, that's true."

The Indian rises and walks away, his footsteps entirely inaudible. The passerby takes a seat on the bench beside the woman. She passes a paint-stained hand through her hair, casually.

"Well, what do you say we rehearse our backgrounds very briefly, Bub, one for the other. Mine, of course, will contain references to the castle in which you will no doubt be interested."

"Sure," he says. "My story is born in the U.S.A., don't like to work too hard, live alone (married and divorced the one time), no army, a fondness for women, considering them mysterious in every way. For instance, those good-looking overalls you're wearing there, I like those a lot in spite of the fact they baffle me completely. I do like where it says 'United States Government' there on the back."

She says, "Why, thank you. As for me, well, my father

played the violin. The story goes he heard it first on Berlin radio while still quite young, while the hair on his head was still the hair of a peach, yessir. And he was taken by the sound. The stinging edge of the old music. Haunted, that's the old man, the old fluff haunted by the power of music and passed it along, passed it along, pledged himself and the selves of the sired (that was done in those days, don't you know) to the instrument and the art. Unhappily for me, the pledge didn't take. I'm a painter."

"You went for the brush?"

"I despise imagination, Bub, that's what. It taunts a person, constantly reporting a person's failure. But the brush? No, don't use no brush. Don't nobody use no brush nowadays far as I can tell—Peter Reginato, for example, give up the brush utterly."

"Well," he says. "I had heard that. He's working with Ko-Rec-Type now, right?"

"And we in the government service, why, we approve of his choice is what. We think he done a fine thing, considering."

The man is moving a lot. Moving his arms and legs, his head, twisting his neck this way and that, crossing and recrossing his legs.

"Speaking of which," she says, "What it comes to is a small salary in the area thirty G's, something like that."

She's staring at him.

He says, "I see. Me, I do research, I keep my eyes open for the odd little telltale something—like these eyes of yours." He points at her eyes. "Tell me, this stuff around here, the shadows and such—this is true shadow and not false shadow?"

"Natural consequence of the government life, don't you know. As I have led and am leading still. La life bureaucratique," she says. "I suppose it causes a person to yearn somewhat. A person yearns for marriage and family, maybe a small place in the hills—love of the seasons and love of the seagulls, that sort of a thing, a spaniel, some special spaniel between the self and the other."

"The other?"

"That would be you, Bub. Exactly—that's my bug right over yonder, see? The green devil."

"Very pretty, very nice," he says.

"I can get in that bug o' mine and ride and ride, to a great castle on the river, a sporting event . . ."

"So you only wear this uniform to work, then? Everyone there have a uniform like this?"

"Got my name on it here, see, sewn on so all the other painters will know my name when we confront, as, say, over a particularly troublesome hue, a blue, perhaps, me being blue-fixated, a fine artist, a weaver of the cloth that kills." She is moved by this characterization of herself. "And you, Bubster, what are you? Occupationally speaking?"

"I am a friend of women."

"Nothing wrong in that, nothing at all. The world has too few friends, and of that number too few are for the women. The women get a raw deal, all in all. You studied somewhere, I presume?"

"Department of Divinity, San Antonio School of Women. I'm ABD."

"Aren't we all," she says.

He seems proud and she seems pleased. They sit

together next to the fountain, which is the centerpiece of the mall, in the mall's apse, and gaze for a few moments at the shoppers carrying packages, trails of gift-wrap and glitter overflowing the shoppers' bags, and while they gaze they listen to the big happy music coming out of speakers mounted in the ceiling of the mall, and they are satisfied in some wholly immeasurable yet noticeable way, they are content to play their small part in the picture, their part in the scene. After a few minutes of this pleasure, the woman reopens the conversation.

"So let's get this straight, Bub, about you and the women."

"I am the man who loves women."

"One of many, it would seem. You know, Bub, my brother recently went to New York City for the first time in his life, and when he came back he said he hated it, that it was a zoo."

"Thousands say that, hundreds of thousands."

"But, you see, the women in New York are as slick as the lovely white shine on a smiling egg, sunny-side up."

"Exactly," he says.

"For the women in New York are as sweet as the stone sucked in the drama, Bub," she says. "They do, however, get the odd runny nose. And that redness on the skin when the weather goes bad, my brother says."

"You have a point."

"And the teeth are not the best teeth," she says.

The passerby is in one hundred percent agreement. "I agree."

"And there is an unpleasant scraggly look about the hair in many cases, a look suggesting the toilet floor."

"Hang on, now—"

"Sorry. I'm overdoing it. I am, I am, and I am. Looks aren't everything, are they? You are absolutely correct, and how could I have been so thoughtless on the hair?"

"You've got nothing against New York," he says.

"Nor Ohio," she says. "Where the women are one and all car hops—it is the great dream of Ohio."

"I love them just the same," he says.

"Your job," she says.

"My heart, too, I'm afraid. Listen, say . . . there are a lot of lesbians in the government, are there not?"

"I don't mind the odd lesbian, Bub," she says.

"I didn't want to suggest you did," he says.

"A lesbian can be a friend, a true and vital friend to you and to me," she says.

"Absolutely, I agree. She is, after all, still a woman."

"With verifiable needs, sexual and otherwise."

She looks at him with a sudden searching look, causing some unease. He looks away. The afternoon has dimmed, the bright sky in the clerestory of the mall is not as bright as it was, the crowd is thinner, the clerks begin to gather at the entrances to their shops.

"My brother's a painter too," she says. "He paints little animals with mechanical feet."

"Mechanical mice, you mean?"

"No, no, we're in the dragon and tiny ape field. All the time I wish I painted what he paints—he paints everything but the red thing you wind up when you wind up the animals," she says.

"You paint the red thing, then?"

"Right, right."

This gives him pause. "I see. That's not a lot of painting, is it?"

"It's limiting, I agree. Still, it's what I got and no use bitching. Injustice is all the way of it, yes?"

"But you can express yourself on the red thing, can't you? You are allowed?"

"Absolutely. I can express myself utterly as long as it's red and you can wind it," she says.

"And your husband?"

"What? Oh—saw the ring, did you? Yes, a painter too. Actually he's a chemist, but he paints nights and weekends. Paints all his own beakers—little pastorals, chicken at the swimming hole, that sort of thing. He's at the lab painting right now, tonight."

"I see. Well, everybody paints these days; I even paint a bit—pictures of women."

"Lord have mercy," she says.

"I hate it," he says.

"Big personal anxiety attaches itself to the practitioner, Bub. You got to pay the piper."

"I mean, sometimes . . ." He looks away, gazes.

"You want to be a plain old friend of women, there with your dangerous cap on your slick hair, damp in perpetuity?"

"Cap or hair?" he says.

"I haven't finished about my father," she says. "I was brought up on a sound stage, people all around outfitted with foolish and ill-conceived Roman garb, but they were all bakers, really, eating rye bread and remembering stickball the way great artists do, as a stupid game which has come, for them, to speak for what has been lost."

"I see," he says, "a certain manufactured enrichment of an undeserving past."

"My point, exactly," she says. "Castle and magic

linked to the old man, I'm afraid, or some other man, always, inevitably, like a man carrying a small white dog in his hat, like a man with a locket containing the future of Saxony."

"Your father, the violinist?"

"Made models of Greek architecture, Bub, in green modeling clay, my clay, poached from my set of clays, leaving me with the red alone, the bloody amazing cantankerous swine!"

"What happened to the blue?"

"Never gave me no blue. Blue was not included with my set." She lurches forward, bent at the waist, looking at his foot. "Hey! What's that you doin' with your foot?"

"Sorry," he says.

"Keep in mind you're the other up to this point, Bub. You don't want to overbear."

"Sorry," he says. "Look at those clerks gathering there: aren't they the sorriest-looking bunch of human beings you ever saw?"

"On the other hand," she says. "Maybe we ought to retire to the castle, get on with our exploration of the possible."

"What about your husband?"

"I told you already, La Husband is at his easel."

"What about your brother?"

"Busy with a new triptych called *The Girl Who Loved Minor Poet's Knees*, a dramatic rendering of unequal love." She smiles a provocative smile. "I'll tell you what—if we go up there, you get to wear his uniform, huh? That is, if you don't mind being called Slippers."

"Slippers?"

"He's a dancing man."

"What about the injun?"

"Whoa," she says. "I get the feeling you're dragging your feet here, Bub. Get up and walk along with me here and I'll tell you a story. Look there at your watch, see? What's the matter you, anyway? See this name here? See this chest? What's the matter you?"

They walk. At the glass entrance to the mall they stand, each with a hand on the door. Outside, at the curb, two young women are bundled thick and tight against the night chill. The wind comes through the crack between the door he's holding and the door she's holding, and the watchman's soft steps approach.

"Well, Bub? You're a painter and I'm a painter and what could be more natural than for two painters like us to go over to my place and do a little scumbling?"

"The thing is, I don't want to see your skin, to tell you the truth. Plus, I got to go to league."

"League? You got to go to *league?*"

"Bowling."

"Forget it, Bub. I'm gonna show you my book of cowboys."

"I think I'd really better not."

"Got lesbians in it," she says.

"Ah," he says.

"You're just a little scared is all, nothing wrong in that," she says. "Does have its limits charmwise, don't you see, but c'mon over anyway and we'll have us a good time, no question. What, you got some kind of low-grade depression prevents you from functioning proper? Can't adore the confounding and the uncanny, that the idea?"

"Maybe we could meet tomorrow?" he says.

"What is that, a flair for melodrama? You got responsibilities now, Bub. You want to come along and carry out your duties and responsibilities, that's what. You want to pay up."

"Maybe I could lend you some cash?"

"Maybe you could explain this unnatural reticence with respect to consummation of the encounter, Bub. See, I'm beginning to get upset here, and it might be a good idea if you offered some explanation before I wang ya."

"Well . . . Hey, look! There goes Spinning! And what's that he's got in his hand? Looks like a pistol."

"Mister Microphone, Bub. He's gonna tell the world."

"I thought he was a friend of yours."

"They're all friends. I give 'em Mister Microphones for Christmas. See, I got a wagon full of Mister Microphones."

"Oh."

"Well?" she says.

She waits for his explanation, tapping fingers.

"I just thought, you know, that I might be required," he says, "in the course of events, perhaps in the shank of the evening, I might be asked, then, in the normal way of things, to, as it were, *perform*, and—well, don't you see, I'm just a simple friend of women, that's all—I mean, that's the end of it, the limit, the outer edge."

"Shoot," she says.

"It's true," he says.

"I don't believe it. A woman offers you a little friendship and companionship and peership and collegiality and maybe a castle into the bargain, and bam! you go off imagining things."

"Well, I could call you on the telephone," he says. "I

could do that, go home and call you right away and we could talk all night long, into the wee hours."

"Hot dog and that's swell, Bub."

"I do like you," he says.

"You find me attractive?"

"Your eyes are real nice," he says.

"Forget the eyes, will you? What about the rest of me? What about my tiny little waist, for example? My curves? My other attributes? My skin like clear water?"

He says, "Most of the time, for me, skin looks better in photographs. I'm sorry to say."

"The iconographic effect of D-76? Known to the trade for centuries? But, it's a lie. Skin in pictures isn't real skin at all."

"Yeah, well, that would be among its advantages, don't you see," he says.

"It feels crummy to the touch," she says. "And usually it's not very big, not big enough."

"If you bring it very close to the eye it's big—blinding and big as a bulldozer."

"Ah!" She steps back a pace. "So you are involved with the life of the mind, then? You are willing to sacrifice the body?"

"The life of the body is no good."

"A theme now dog-eared, I'm afraid. But never mind, I acknowledge it—one of the acceptable themes. What do you say we go, uh, sit in the car awhile? Maybe talk this over?"

"You won't hurt me?"

"Why, you really are some kind of fastidious weasel, aren't you?" she says.

They walk to the cars. By utter coincidence his car is next to her car, and the two cars are the only remaining cars in the huge parking lot, back to front and side by side, his brown, a sedan, hers a VW, in the great black lot cluttered with yellow lines and spotted here and there with flat green light. They get into her car. Back at the building the ruddy face of the night watchman is pressed against the glass.

"I'd like to come over," he says. "I really would, but, well—do you understand at all?"

"You're a friend of women," she says.

"I got to go," he says.

"Looky, Bub, you can take it or leave it, it's all the same to me. I mean a castle's a castle where I come from. I can go home and play with my PVC pipe is what I can do, watch the TV and think about my beautiful mother is what I can do. Play the oboe. The oboe was my mother's axe—range of three octaves, penetrating and poignant sound, haunting my father from the French. Perfect for me." She stares at his shirt front. "Say, what's this on your shirt here?"

"Where?"

"This spot. Looks like ice cream."

"Yeah, well, I had a cone."

"You what?"

"Had a cone, you know, had a cone."

"You had a cone. Bub, that's good, that's rich. That tells the story. See, I thought it was a Captain Don button, something like that."

"Captain Don?"

You know, the buttons they give away at the grocery. They throw 'em in your sack when you're not looking, slip 'em in with your change so you put 'em away and find 'em the next day—damnedest things."

"No. I had a cone."

"I see," she says.

"You know, your eyes are really silver out here."

"One of the many wonderful colors available to me by birth, natural born, all the time changing so as to provide my companions with the visual stimuli, Bub, just another bit of trickery to twist your resolve—your thick resolve—although in this case and at the present time you may forget it because I am tired, very exhausted, and it's going to rain, I think."

"Listen," he says. "I'm sorry about this, about everything."

"Hey! It's O.K. It's perfectly fine. Leave me to muscle up to my castle alone while you keep open your eyes and keep up the work, the fine work, well, that's good, that's O.K., and you don't want to think about tomorrow, about discharge of your proper responsibilities, why, Bub, that's your business—punch the lock, will you? Remember this: tomorrow we're closed. Tomorrow you are pole meat and we're slammed up tight as teeth."

PERFECT
THINGS

Jerry Jordan was upset the morning he found out his wife, Ellen, had a lover. The first thing he did was refuse to carry the army-green garbage sack to the edge of their driveway for the men to pick up, thinking that if he did not carry it, it would not be carried, and that this would be a clear natural consequence of her action not lost on Ellen. As it turned out, Ellen, in a bit of drama Jerry characterized as "endearingly small," took the garbage herself, making a great show of it, banging the overstuffed sack into walls and doorjambs, groaning under its weight, pausing to rest and catch her breath more often than conceivably necessary—it put him in mind of some biblical story, something with Moses and a number of huge, sand-colored rocks. Jerry watched and listened, his feet propped on the butcher-block coffee table just where they had been when, moments before, Ellen had told him about Toby. Toby was a friend of a friend—she'd started with that. Somebody familiar, even close, but somehow obscured. Not a friend of a friend of his, but a friend of a friend of hers, meaning not only did *she* have friends that were not also his, but *they* had friends she took as lovers.

Jerry did not know his next move. He waited for her to return from the long march to the end of the drive, then sat on the couch and watched as she fetched her breakfast to the table, trip after trip for coffee, toast, utensils, newspapers. She seemed to be ignoring him.

"So what do you think you're doing?" he said, crossing the room to the table.

"Eating," she said. "Toast?" She waved a slice of toast at him.

"Marbles?" he said, mimicking her wave. "What I want to know is what you think you're doing slipping over to some kid's house at three in the afternoon for a little hanky-panky." "Hanky-panky" had just come out. He hadn't thought about it, and it didn't describe what he saw in his head when he thought about Ellen and her lover, and it gave the impression, he thought, of a man hopelessly out of touch—it was his mother's expression, something from another era. He was so self-conscious about this unfortunate choice of words that he could not even look up from the tabletop, from a point just alongside his peach placemat where a triangular bit of jelly caught the light and shined. "Or whatever you people call it now," he said, thinking the effort to separate himself from her and from such behavior might salvage his ground—making the behavior so foreign to him that he could not even call it by an appropriate and timely name, thus cutting her off from their life together, isolating her in a sea of her own bad faith. He was immediately aware, however, that the isolation cut both ways, reminding him of the distance she'd strayed from what he had theretofore taken as their mutually satisfying marriage.

Ellen said, "I don't know what I'm doing, if anybody cares." She had her cup in two hands, poised before her chin, precisely square, he noticed, as if some internal gyroscope maintained for her limbs at all times a perfect equilibrium, a perfect relation with the horizon.

Jerry nodded. A minimal nod. Two short up-and-downs of the head, total movement perhaps half an inch. Just enough to register her reply, to say that he heard, and to suggest he was thinking about it. What he in fact thought was how pretty she was, and how surprising that after eleven years of marriage he still thought that. "You don't know," Jerry said, repeating it to buy some time. It was his turn, and he had spent the moment thinking about how attractive she was and he needed to come up with his next line, so he repeated that she didn't know, again hoping the repetition would put her on defense, suggest that her answer was so inadequate that it taxed imagination. Of course, it was a rhetorically ordinary move that he knew would have little effect other than holding his right of next remark. Still, if she felt just a touch guilty, if she felt she weren't operating in good faith in the conversation, she might attempt to revise and extend her answer. That was a possibility.

He decided to try and improve his position. "You always know," he said. "Cut me some line, will you?"

"I'm tired," Ellen said. "I'm old. I'm lonely most of the time. I don't have any fun. I despise all of your friends and I'm never comfortable with them. I'm almost forty, can you believe that?"

He nodded again, picked up the jelly with the tip of his forefinger, and wiped it onto the edge of his plate. He had two thoughts. The first was that she was changing the turf, expanding it, and he wasn't sure what to make of that. They'd gone from confrontation to revelation—they were going to play Tell the Truth, which, of course, obligated him. The second thought was, he imagined, somehow extrapolated from the tone of her remark. It was, What if she begins to wear a muumuu around the house?

"Me too," he finally said, thinking that it was not only true, but also safe. He was nearer forty than she was.

Ellen took a minute, then went on. "I get up every day and do stuff I don't want to do," she said. "I grind coffee beans, for example. I don't know why I do that. Why can't I just have regular coffee, Maxwell House or something? But, no. I get up and I come in here"—she pointed toward the kitchen—"I get the coffee out of the freezer, I put the beans in the grinder, I grind 'em." She made a helpless gesture with her hands. "I hate it. I hate the way it sounds. Every morning. It's awful."

"I know what you mean," Jerry said. "For me it's getting the paper. I walk out there on the pea-gravel concrete there and it hurts my feet, and I always wonder who's watching, if anybody is, and I'm out there in this sick-looking robe I've had since Nixon—I don't know why I don't just get another robe, you know what I mean? How hard can it be?"

He took the coffee bean story as a signal that she wanted to turn down the wick, to diminish the gravity of the complaint—her complaint, and his by association—by facing it with this silly example, and he wondered if, after the broad charges she opened with—the business about friends and loneliness—she had not already softened some, cooled off, decided in the short space of the minute or so he'd taken to reply that things weren't so bad.

"I'll get you a robe," she said. "What color?"

That had to be read, he thought, as conciliatory. He decided to go the opposite way, take a hard line. "I don't want a robe. That's the point. Why do I have to have a robe? I hate robes. They're so stupid. I don't even want to see another robe."

"White," she said. "You'll feel like Macho Camacho."

Clever. She'd set him up for the macho joke, of which he was, unmistakably, the butt, inasmuch as she had hours before seen fit to seek sexual gratification elsewhere, with a young man, a student, and, at that, a Latin. Jerry watched the slits in the Levolors brighten as the sun finally rose above the roof next door and came down their own east-facing kitchen wall. He noticed that the blinds were cranked the wrong way, with the lower edges of the slats toward the inside rather than the outside, and he got up to fix that. It was something that Ellen did every night, turn the blinds that way, because she liked the way they looked better when the concave part of the slat was facing out. This in spite of the fact that she was always first in the kitchen in the morning and had to face first the harshness of the light that penetrated the blinds when they were closed that way. The morning did not seem to bother her at all. Jerry was the opposite. He agreed that the blinds looked better at night when they were closed downside in, but he thought they ought to be downside out at bedtime, so that in the morning there wasn't this ugly smear of light when the sun hit.

"I hate it that you leave the blinds this way," he said, going into the kitchen.

"I know," she said. "You told me. But I hate the blinds. I hate curtains too. As a matter of fact, I don't like windows all that much. I wish we could just put chunks of plywood up there, know what I mean?"

"That's a great idea," he said.

"It's what I feel," she said.

"So—you really like sleeping with this guy or what?" He was disappointed with "sleeping with"—why hadn't he gone for sleaze? He'd been thinking sleaze—details, fleshy stuff—why had he backed away? He decided he was afraid to show himself, show that he cared not about the depression, the malaise she might be suffering, not about the reasons for her choice, or the motivation, or the vulnerability that led her to it, not about fear, or need, or any genuine or humane aspect of her situation, but about the nickel-and-dime stuff. He was back in high school. He wanted it to sting. "You like it, huh?" he said.

Ellen gave him a steady look, her features unmoved, at rest, the flatness of the gaze telling him she thought he was dull, cheap, disgusting, and pathetic. Then she moved her mouth into a nasty-looking small smile, small enough so that it could not be mistaken for a real smile, and she said, "He's very good."

This reminded him that he did not want to hear the truth about his wife and her twenty-four-year-old boy-friend.

Instantly, he hated her. Dim-witted, wedded to sensation, a masseuse's dream. Why wasn't she lame, like him?

Immune to the physical, bound instead to talk and fantasy, stuff that could turn pigs-in-blankets into hot tamales—lightning cracking between two unexpected parts of two unsuspecting bodies? He was vulnerable here. Felt weak and defensive. But—Toby? His aggression had backfired on him and now he looked at Ellen, who was sitting across the table feeling sorry for him, for his . . . limitations. It made him want to tear his skin off, but he resisted the temptation to say something about dogs, which he knew would be inflammatory, out of line, which might terminate the conversation, shut her up semipermanently, and instead nodded again, taking his medicine, accepting his failure, or, at least, appearing to accept his failure, or appearing to accept her idea of his failure.

He said, with only slight bitterness, "I'll bet he is," and he was proud of it, of the way it had come out. The tone—the content was hot, but the presentation lacked affect—disdain paired with disinterest. She would know, of course, which was meant and which was camouflage, but the disentangling might slow her down, might even seed some doubt.

Jerry was picturing Ellen in the heat of a video version of lovemaking, or trying to picture her, for they had grown so comfortable together, so matched, and so far from lust, that the image of her in passionate embrace, perspiration rolling off her shining cheeks, eyes glazed, lips ballooned into pillowy sexual membrane—this wouldn't quite come to him. The problem, he imagined, in a nutshell.

"So what do you want to know?" Ellen said. She had repositioned herself in the chair, and she was pouting.

"You want to know why? Why is because it came up. Maybe because we could be doing better, you and me. We used to do better. I don't know why we don't anymore. I feel left out. Of everything. You name it, I feel left out of it. The War in Vietnam, for example. The Me Generation. Farm Aid. The New German cinema. The BMW crowd. I mean, where's *my* 505? Hawaiian shirts— I wanted to wear one of those, a couple of 'em. The sexual revolution. Making ends meet—remember that? You get a dump and clean it up and everything? I can't do that. I get to choose between a hundred-and-fifty-thousand-dollar house and a hundred-and-eighty-thousand-dollar house—what fun is that? Or I can be postmodern, read *Metropolis*, pay five grand for a chair, eight fifty for dinner. It's all under control, right? I hate it. I hate the lawn, Jerry, know what I mean?"

Jerry studied her face and decided that this remark was a sincere expression of disenchantment with the success they had shared.

"I don't like the lawn either," he said.

This was true. He had, on more than one occasion, thought exactly that he hated the lawn. He remembered staring out the window at the lawn, particularly the back lawn, and thinking how much he hated it. So now he tried to remember how he had gotten over that. But he couldn't remember a thing, he could barely remember what the lawn looked like, and he felt she had twisted the talk around to be about something it wasn't really about. That made him angry, so he said, "But I don't go out picking up college kids for amusement just because the lawn disgusts me."

"Why not?" she said.

He thought she ought to be feeling guilty, but, watching her, he could see that she didn't feel the slightest bit guilty, or, if she did, she wasn't letting him see it, which wasn't fair. Not only was it not fair, it wasn't kind, or compassionate, or good-hearted. In fact, her question was so perfectly weightless that it was like some terrible explosive accidentally swallowed.

"We don't do that because that's the definition of rabbits," he said, and immediately wished he hadn't. There were so many things wrong with it. It was clumsy, didn't quite fit as an answer—and why hadn't he put some lower life-form in for rabbits? Rabbits were so cute, inescapably furry and flop-eared—how could rabbits be bad? But he couldn't think of another, lesser animal with the same kind of reputation, and he realized the point wouldn't be made at all without them, so he let it go and tried to think of some other way to say to Ellen that the release suggested by "why not?" was, in a way, the problem, for if you had no more restraint than that implicit in the question, if you were already leaning in the direction of doing whatever it was, so that the burden of argument was placed on the dissuasion side of things, then you had not much restraint at all, about as much as a hot monkey—he liked that "hot monkey" part, and wondered if it was too soon after the rabbits to throw it in.

She, meanwhile, had begun to clear away her place at the table—the plate with the orange peel on it, the plate that had held her toast, the plate with the husk of her honeydew melon, her small glass of milk and larger glass of water, the three crumpled napkins she had accumulated during the meal, the butter-encrusted knife, and the four bottles containing the various pills she took every morning at breakfast, the pills themselves remaining on the tablecloth in a tight, multicolored group.

"You're kind of a complex molecule, here," Jerry said, circling a finger toward her mat and the debris she was clearing away.

She stopped at the kitchen door and turned to stare at him, her eyes narrowed, a bemused expression on her face. She didn't say a word, just looked.

He wondered why things seemed to accumulate around her wherever she lit for more than a moment—in order to watch TV she had to have a glass of bottled water, the bottle of cold water itself for possible refills (not the bottle the water actually came in, since that was a one-gallon plastic jug which wouldn't fit in the refrigerator, and thus couldn't be chilled, but an intermediate container, a two-liter ripple-plastic French spa-water bottle, which would fit in the lowest door tray of the refrigerator and was constantly refilled from the larger container kept under the sink), a diet Coke, her cigarettes, lighter, and ashtray, two newspapers (yesterday's and today's), and at least one magazine to flip through during commercials, Kleenex, a sweater in case things got chilly, one each package of gum and package of breath mints, and miscellaneous other equipment from sewing stuff to ankle weights, depending on the secondary pursuits being pursued right at the moment of the show she was setting out to watch. He hadn't, heretofore, been bothered by it the way he was this morning.

"What about it?" she said. She was out of sight, in the kitchen.

"What about Toby?" Jerry said.

"Toby's a nice boy," she said. "Toby's external to our relationship. In fact, I think you'd like him."

"I don't like him. I never would like him. He could cure spinal meningitis and I wouldn't like him."

"They already cured spinal meningitis," she said.

"I knew that," he said.

"You'd like him."

This was typical of his conversations with Ellen. She had her ideas, inhabited utterly, which for practical purposes could not be addressed. He saw these ideas as at the mercy of dark forces, which is to say that he didn't know what forces there were that would lead to her ideas. He had, of course, tried reason, as he would try again shortly, sure of its failure, confident that she would not alter her thought on the matter at all, but bound nevertheless to make the effort, to point out to her that it was unlikely that he, the wronged party, would, under the present circumstances, or any other circumstances subsequent to those present ones, *like* Toby. Toby was her lover. Toby was to her what he was not. Toby was an intruder in their otherwise satisfactory, or thought-to-be-satisfactory, marriage, the intruder whose appearance suggested that the marriage was not satisfactory at all, that it was, in fact, stupid and empty.

"I hate his guts," Jerry said.

He didn't feel this, he felt nothing like it; in fact, he didn't have much feeling about Toby one way or the other. What he did feel was much in love with Ellen, more in love than he had been in a long time. He thought about the way she smiled, the huskiness in her voice sometimes, the goofy way she had of laughing when she was really amused, the peculiar rituals upon which she insisted, the trouble she had dressing from time to time and the way she got angry if he tried to help, tried to suggest that the yellow flats were probably never going to walk comfortably beneath the purple-and-black shirt. He was flooded with images of his wife at her most lovely, which was not necessarily coincident with her most beautiful, although it often was, but a separate thing entirely, a capacity she had for breaking his heart at moments when the tide of things seemed to run against her and she, recognizing this, gave up, shaking her head and reminding herself of the foolishness of attempting to impose order on a thing so disorderly as ordinary life. Those were the times he liked her most, and, since the idea she now championed—that he would like her newly taken lover—was so dumb, and since she had some sense left, and since she was standing there and he could see the recognition of the silliness of her position closing over her like the shadow of a rain cloud sliding over a sun-dappled pond, her face beginning to register the wrong-ness of the idea, expanding with it into a smile and then a wide, self-mocking grin, Jerry Jordan realized that this was one of those times that he loved her most.

"I guess you're right," Ellen said.

"Still," Jerry said. "There he is."

She came to the kitchen door and leaned against the jamb, nodding. She was eating lemon yogurt out of a paper tub. "Yep," she said. "Like a hatchet buried deep in the soft flesh of our relationship."

"Yes," he said.

"I see that," she said.

He watched her carefully as she cleared the remaining breakfast dishes and prepared for her morning workout.

She was splendidly young and sexy in yellow nylon
shorts and a mint-green T-shirt, minicassette strung dan-
gerously at her waist, earphones in place, blue-leather
ankle weights belted like huge, stylish watches to her
wrists. He went out with her, stood on the ten-by-fifteen-
foot white pine deck as she strode purposefully away,
arms already pumping, embarked on what his father
would have called her constitutional.

He was staring at a redbird when she made the block
for the first time and waved in that bothered way people
who are preoccupied wave when they feel it is their duty.

BLACK TIE

At midnight Paul says, "Shh! Be quiet!" He shakes Katherine's shoulder; she jerks awake. She is beautifully draggled, her hair lank, sparkling across her temple to her cheek.

"What?" she says.

"Shh! Quiet! I heard something."

"Paul," she says, removing his hand from her shoulder, "there are no burglars, there is no junkie, the escapees are all escaping in some other direction. Less than four percent of the population is burglarious—the odds are good. Go to sleep."

He pushes a hand at her face, wags a finger back and forth, accidentally catches her on the chin.

This makes her angry.

"The criminals are interested in diamonds and animals, but as you suspect, Paul, there are many with eyes only for you." She goes to the bathroom and returns with a Sucrets, three aspirin, a glass of salt water, a heating pad, a jar of Vicks VapoRub, two Rolaids, a tablespoon of Gelusil, a wet washcloth, and an antiphlogistine. "Here," she says.

He is quiet for a minute, then says, "I feel better already."

"Ah, don't be silly," Katherine says. "I'm beginning to think you aren't serious."

"I know," he says. "I know. Does everyone else know?"

"Who's paying attention?"

"Oh . . . forces of evil, governments, friends."

She looks at Paul with a curious look: "What is evil?"

"Let's go out," he says.

"Out? Where? It's dark! No."

They get into the car and drive out Telegraph Street toward the bridge, the country, the fields of corn and the flocks of crow. The midnight air is thick and heavy and wet; Katherine rolls her window halfway up; the pearl highway lamps hang above them and slide by, green flying circles over the hood and into the glass, one after another.

Katherine says, "I liked freeways until they became popular. They're nice in movies. Want to go to a movie? No, I guess it's too late. We should take a trip, Paul. Do you want to take a trip? No, I guess not. Are we going to sing on this drive?"

"You feel O.K.?" Paul says.

"You mean, do I need a change? Is my life unfull? Should I get involved? Well, no. That view has fallen from favor. Meaning must be found in the self, Paul, only I looked there already."

"With small success," he says. "We could use some singing."

"Recognition of our signal, anyway."

She sticks Paul in the side with the tire gauge, using it like a false knife the blade of which slips into the handle when the knife is pressed into service.

"Maybe riches," Katherine says, "and . . . slaves?"

She puts the tire gauge away, takes out the map, opens it, puts it in her lap, and holds it there while she gets a Pentel out of the glove compartment. Rolls her window down. Turns on the map light.

"Alignment?" she says. "Is that it?"

"Formerly, I was loath to align. I'm still sort of loath to align. I mean, I don't know."

"Let me get this straight, Paul," she says. "I want to get this straight. You desire alignment, so-called. However, you want to specify . . . what? Income? Caste?"

She marks a bomb pattern on the map, makes airplane noises, flies her hand over the target, runs into bad weather, drops the bombs.

"How I feel. I want to specify how I feel."

"Well, how do you feel?"

"Better," he says. "I guess I feel a whole lot better than I used to. Still, we've smiled and slept, and laughter's been ours, but inadequate. We've tried bitterness and public angst, we've tried to not pay attention, we've told carnival jokes and fiddled the bull fiddle—with twenty-odd fingers into the act you'd think our double stop would be out of sight, but you'd be wrong. Our double-stop technique is the envy of no responsible players. Piano people only nod, graciously; tenormen hoot and honk and hack and hum. How do I feel? I feel we will not learn."

She sighs: "The way we were born, what we have done."

Paul turns the steering wheel of the car so that the car rolls right into the bright lights of an all-night filling station.

"Where are we?" Katherine asks.

"I smell gas," Katherine says.

The attendant stares at Katherine. He is sitting on a stool in his glass booth on the island where the gas pumps are. Paul stares at the attendant. When Katherine goes to the ladies' room, the attendant watches her go. Then Paul asks for two dollars' worth of Regular gas.

"Sure, okay," the attendant says. "Regular gas."

Paul gives the man a five-dollar bill, then walks to the station's edge where the concrete, lovely and smooth, gives way to weeds, piled tires, a sweeping horizon of poles, black rectangles, high skeletons, hot distant lights, and running wires. Paul stands there.

The attendant hands Paul three dollars and a strip of Black Gold Trading Stamps and an eight-ounce glass with a rendering of the National Dance Company of Siberia in action frosted on its side.

"Thanks," Paul says.

"Sure, sure," the attendant says. "Where you headed?"

"Carnegie-Mellon, if the weather holds."

The attendant nods and Paul looks at the sky. Katherine returns with two RC Colas, three candy bars, and a package of peanuts. As she gets into the car the attendant bends to watch. She waves the peanuts at him.

"You got a ways to go yet," the attendant says to Paul. "Best take it slow."

Paul thanks him and starts the car. Katherine puts an unwrapped Snickers in Paul's mouth, an open RC Cola on the seat between his legs, and she drops the peanuts on the glove compartment door.

"The thing that has been lost," she says, "is faith—you remember faith? But, Paul, it's not so bad; we could ease into it—a book, a fiery fire; intrigue, immorality, faraway places—it might work."

"No, no, no, no," he says.

"Oh, right. I forgot. We must cast our seed carefully. However, Paul, the wayside can be quite pleasant in spots. Look there! And . . . what's that? You see, a flight of nightbirds. How pretty. We'll be all right, Paul. We can start, we can build a new life, a new time. Where is imagination? Spirit? Will?"

"Frittered," he sighs, "away."

"Oh, pooh," she says.

He turns off the highway, down an unmarked road; dust rises into the air. Paul stops half a mile in, facing the highway; the night is full of cries, howls, jingles and jangles. Short drifts of wind bring the sizzle of tires on the highway.

"We don't belong here, Paul," she says. "It's fake."

He opens his door and puts his foot in the doorjamb and takes a drink of RC and rolls his head back and gargles his throat.

She says: "Makes me nervous, you know? Feels fishy. We can't stay here, Paul. We have to go back. Nobody lives here. We don't live here."

The panel lights glow a favorable green.

Paul says: "Some troubles are worse than ours, probably. I like it here, Katherine, it's nice—these fields, the dark, the breeze, the size."

"The battery," she says.

"You're lovely, Katherine. You're lovely and you're right—the battery. Yet here, our failure seems small;

we're not doing so bad, we have a grace here on our knees—screw the battery. Let's get stranded. Let's stay."

"Bugs."

"I forgot about bugs."

Paul takes the key out of the lock and pushes the light knob and flips the blinker back and forth and rocks the wheel and puts his heel on the black button in the doorjamb.

"We should help somebody."

"How about me?" she says. She gets out of the car and walks around in the field. Then she comes up on Paul's side of the car and twists his foot.

"Sometimes," he says, "a thing is as beautiful as its name."

"True," she says. "But Paul, your rigor's misplaced. There are only two questions. The first question is: Hope? The second question is: What happened? As to the first question I'd say yes—I mean, what've we got to lose? And on the second and more interesting question, I give up. We're frightened. From fear we infer guilt. And we are the judge, Paul. And we are the jury. We are the prosecuting attorneys, the witnesses, and the court-appointed lawyers for the defense. We are the Department of Corrections, the slam. And the warden and the guards guarding. And Paul darling, when the tomahawk swings, it's our hand in sweat on the shank, us on the block."

"Discomfort," he says. "Responsibility."

"I think so, yes. Plain old responsibility."

"Well," he says, "I don't think what has been lost has been lost at all, Katherine, I think it's been hidden."

"Ahh, don't be silly, Paul. Start the car."

He starts the car. She tosses her RC into the ditch and

gets in the car and they drive to the highway and head home. Katherine puts away the tire gauge, and the map, and the pliers, and the Pentel.

The moon is full.

At the house she helps Paul close the garage door. They stand in the driveway: she hugs him.

"This is O.K.," she says. "Wind, street—coming home, Paul. Not a bad finish; not a bad world. I mean, right?"

Paul says: "I like you, Katherine."

"And why not? I walk, talk, ambulate, somnambulate, fox trot—why not like me?"

PARENTS

"**C**an't hear you, Agnes," he lies. Heinz is watching blackbirds walk around in the yard. The birds are pecking at the new snow, trying to get at what is underneath.

Agnes comes out of the bathroom snapping the fly of her jeans. She has washed her hands and now wipes them on the rim of the flowered couch. "I said you'd make a lousy woman. It's hard. You have no idea."

"I'm lonely," Heinz says.

Agnes stands behind his chair watching the birds. "You had telephone calls yesterday."

He ignores her. "You don't ever say anything interesting."

It is snowing. The bird tracks in the fresh snow are oddly curved, not tentative. On the street beyond the yard people with bicycles stand under grocery awnings to watch the snow fall.

"So," Agnes says. "It's snowing."

"See what I mean?"

Agnes laughs at him.

"I know," he says. "I had telephone calls yesterday. We probably went to the store not too long ago. I have a sense of history."

She tells him a story about a friend of hers, a lawyer, who once propped a dead animal on a sheriff's porch in a small New England town. When he does not smile Agnes says: "I know. I don't think it's such a good story."

"Let's take a nap," he says, getting up.

They go into the bedroom and get into bed. Agnes falls asleep almost immediately. Heinz cannot sleep and wakes her.

"I can't," he says. "I want to screw. Let's have a baby." As he says it, Heinz notices that it sounds odd, interesting. He is surprised. He has said it just to say something, but, having said it, he means it. "You want to?"

She says: "No. I'll get fixed. It'll just take a minute."

Agnes gets out of the bed, but he tackles her at the bedroom door. They wrestle playfully on the floor until she says: "I mean it, Heinz."

He rolls away. "Oh, shit."

They sit on the floor, leaning against adjacent walls. Agnes looks at Heinz.

"No kid, huh?"

"No."

"Not even because I'm lonely?"

"Don't be stupid."

"Okay."

Later, as he masturbates, he wonders if Agnes hates him doing it, hates him. He does not ask, however, because he knows that if he asks they will have to discuss their sex for two hours, beginning at the beginning.

Also, he knows how Agnes feels.

At dinner Agnes says: "I want an electric mixer." She is reading the night paper and Heinz imagines that there is an advertisement for electric mixers in the paper, on the page that she is reading or on another page she has already read. He hands her a striped tumbler of orange juice with ice in it and, in doing so, moves around the dining table to see if what he imagines is correct.

"How much?" he asks.

"Twenty-eight, sale from forty."

"I mean, how much do you want it?"

Agnes flattens the paper, covering the sketch of the mixer with her arm. "How much is necessary?"

Heinz sits down. "Sorry."

For four years in the oilfield at Miri, Sarawak, in northeast Borneo, Agnes lived with her first husband, Pete, a Shell Oil engineer, and cooked over wood fire. Now, in the matter of kitchen appliances, she is very touchy.

"You can get it for me tomorrow," Agnes says. "Downtown. Third floor. Go on your lunch."

"I may not go to work tomorrow. How do I look?" He leans across the table, pushing his face into the light of the remaining bulb in the chandelier.

"Your skin is spongy."

"Spongy," he repeats, sitting down. He has noticed how white her teeth are and is puzzled because his own teeth are not at all white. "I have a feeling my father is sick."

"I want the mixer."

•

They go to a movie, a Disney production, and Agnes makes notes on a spiral pad using the aisle light to see what she is doing. Later she tells Heinz that the movie is probably based on fact.

In the drugstore Heinz says: "I should be there when my father is sick. That would be the right thing. Do you know about my father?"

"Fruit seller, sold from a cart in the street, in Baltimore, just after he came to this country. A bona fide immigrant. Sang 'Strawberries! Cantaloupes!' and went to night school. Became a rabbi. His brother in the old country made a pot in plastic coat hangers and sent him money. Died in his garden, a rich man."

"I told you."

At the apartment he takes pictures of Agnes holding a fish, ice tongs, a toy bear. She says the pictures make her face look fat. Heinz says they can't throw the pictures away because people will recognize her. "The garbage man, the neighbors," he says.

"Cut off my head," she says.

"I won't know who it is."

"Nobody will."

She gets the scissors and cuts all the heads out of the pictures and seals the heads in an envelope. "Who should I send them to?"

In the morning Agnes puts on her leotard and sits in the middle of the floor doing exercises.

"Remember that song I sang the time we went to Annapolis?"

"Hmm?" He is busy reading.

"The geese were flying, remember? We were driving and singing—you were singing too—and it got cold and suddenly dark."

"What? No, I—no."

She puts a pillow near the wall to do a headstand on. "Heinz, I want to go to that city in Turkey where all the women wear thick gray veils and the streets are so primitive they cut your feet, the one Pete told me about, you know?"

"What's the worst insult in Borneo, Agnes?"

She thinks a minute. "Spitting in a rice bowl. Why?"

She begins swaying side to side, dragging her bare feet on the wall. Light from the window seems to ripple along her legs. Heinz notices that she hasn't shaved.

"C'mon, Heinz, I'm bored."

"Get a subscription to *Smithsonian*."

In the middle of the afternoon, alone in a bar, Heinz twists a beer coaster into a spiral similar to one he has seen in a book about Naum Gabo, his father's book. He does not know what magic Gabo found in the spiral. The waitress, a woman named Angel, bends over his table. "Hey, I got ideas," she says. "You hear?"

"You always got ideas, Angel."

She wipes the tip of a brown-nailed finger over his lips. "I know it, honey. Makes me sad too."

A big guy with sideburns cut like knife blades trots over to see if she's got trouble; she tells him to get buried.

"I like Gladys," the waitress says. "She's a drip, but I like her."

"Agnes," Heinz says. "Me too."

She smiles. "But, on the other hand, you get tired of the nice job, the nice white shirt, the rest of that toy town, why, come see Angel, huh? Angel knows her business backwards and forwards, you hear?" She smiles again. Her teeth are yellow. Polio, she had said once.

"We're gonna have a baby," he says.

The waitress laughs loud. "Well, honey," she says, standing and straightening her bar apron, "you got the BankAmericard."

"Stupid, huh? Yeah. I don't want to, but Agnes thinks it's a terrific idea."

Agnes is watching the afternoon movie when he gets home. The movie is almost over. The wind pushes a tree limb against the window. It has rained and the snow is almost gone. Heinz stands at the window looking for the tracks of the birds from the day before.

"Turn that off and talk to me," he says.

"Oh, Heinz! Come on, this is good."

"No it isn't."

That evening they go to a party given by a friend of hers and Heinz gets drunk and puts his cigarette out on a book. The hostess suggests to Agnes that Heinz might be better off at home. Agnes gets another friend, a football player named Willis, to drive him. "I won't be late," Agnes says as she helps him into the car.

On the way home Heinz explains the problem to Willis, who smiles politely, understands politely. Heinz gets angry and nearly causes an accident.

In order to pacify Heinz, Willis stops at the bar where Angel works and, at Heinz's instruction, offers the waitress a ride.

Angel looks at Heinz, who is in the car, and at the football player. "Do I get a choice?" she says.

Heinz walks home.

He has lost his key and must wait for Agnes before he can get into the apartment. When she arrives he is asleep in the hall. Trying to get up, he trips on the doormat, hits his head on the latch, and cuts a half-inch hole in his cheek. Agnes takes him to the hospital and tells the nurse in Emergency that he has attempted suicide.

"The silly fart," the nurse says. "We'll dress that and seclude him for tonight. The scar won't be bad."

Agnes and the nurse work on the appropriate forms.

"Happens all the time," the nurse says. "Why, had a woman in here once blew her ear off trying to kill herself—crazy bitch."

"He's been despondent," Agnes says. "Lost his job on Friday, third one in eight months. I don't know what we'll do now." She looks at Heinz and winks, but he does not see her. As she leaves he tries to follow, but the nurse signals two orderlies, ex-hippies, to move him into one of the treatment rooms. Through the curtain Heinz sees Agnes hugging the nurse.

At the Chinese restaurant the following afternoon Heinz and Agnes take a booth with green vinyl seats. There is a papier-mâché fountain in the center of the room, and from a speaker somewhere comes a curious American-sounding Oriental music, played on the vibraharp. Agnes orders fish.

"I slept like a log," she says.

"Screw you," he says, although with the bandage what he says is not greatly clear.

"You'd been acting like a baby, I had to do something. I'll tell you what," she says, reaching into her purse and withdrawing a small plastic container, her blue diaphragm case. She gives this to Heinz. "It's up to you."

He points at the object next to his fork, but does not touch it. "Won't fit," he says.

"Shh! Look, there's that kid from the university!" She

grabs his arm and signals a corner table with her eyes.

"What kid! I don't get it."

"Supposed to have killed some girl, campus beauty, it was in the paper—Carl J. Dauphine, twenty-two, of Oak Grove, to stand trial in the brutal slaying of Margaret Costina, nineteen, of Selma. With a television set, one of those little portables."

"Give me a break, will you?"

"No, really, I think I'll go talk to him."

"Great."

Agnes drops her napkin on the red oilcloth and pushes her chair away from the table.

"Agnes!" But it is too late, she is already half across the room.

Heinz tries to appear nonchalant and gazes at the fountain, which spurts green water at intervals. When the food arrives he clears his throat to get Agnes's attention. She turns, then gets up from the table, shaking hands with the slight, dark young man.

Heinz has served the fish. She eats without a word. Finally Heinz says: "Well?"

"Panasonic," she says.

He looks at her in disbelief, and after a minute they both laugh, and on the way back to the apartment she tosses the diaphragm into a bush alongside a street she's never seen before.

SIS

My sister's husband Byron called and asked how I would like it if he stayed a couple days at our place. It was late afternoon and raining again. We'd had rain for days—winter rain, with fine, whitish drops. There was some flooding, trees were down, the power had gone off a couple times. My wife Emily had phoned ten minutes earlier to tell me the oil light in the car was blinking and she was at a Star station getting it checked. I was home walking around in red cotton socks and thinking about starting a fire when he called.

"How about it?" Byron said. He sounded uncertain, I guess because I'd waited too long to say yes.

I said, "Sure, it's fine. Is Janie O.K.?" I was listening to the traffic in the background, trying to figure where he was.

He said Janie was great, and nothing in the world was going on, nothing to worry about, and he was standing in front of a Jr. Mart and thought he'd be over right away and fill me in on the whole deal. Then he hung up before

I could say I'd be looking for him, which is what I'd planned to say.

My sister picked Byron out in a Dallas bar ten years ago, then she married him. From my point of view it was reasons unknown, but she didn't ask me. He's a furry type, if you know what I mean—furry hair, furry beard, furry back you see when you go swimming with him, which I did once, a couple of years ago. He's beady too, around the eyes, which is bad if you're furry. It's a bad combo. I don't know why he doesn't get some kind of treatment. By now he doesn't have a steady job and he watches a lot of old movies on TV, and, to hear Janie tell it, which I do in our weekly phone calls, he's not a lot of fun for her.

It took him twenty minutes to my back door, and he was happy to see me, which made me feel guilty for what I'd thought about him in the interim.

"How-dee," he said when I opened the door. He slapped me on the shoulder, then held his hand there, pushing a little so I'd get out of the way and let him and his bag, which was like a small futon, into my kitchen.

I got out of the way. "Come on in." I slapped his back a couple of times. "Hey! You're a wet boy, aren't you?"

He grinned. "I'm Mr. Wet—where's Em?"

He called my wife Em. It was his invention, nobody else ever called her Em. I said, "She's at a gas station on East Bilbo—car trouble."

"God damn!" he said, making a face like you'd make if thirty people just died in the crash of a light plane at O'Hare, and you were watching it on CNN. You'd watch the live coverage with this face.

He was squishing around the kitchen in soaked running shoes, gray with purple decorations, some brand I didn't recognize, and he was already at the cabinets. "So," he said, yanking a Ziploc bag of candy—M&Ms, Tootsie Roll Pops, orange play peanuts—out of the bread cabinet. "Hey! Jackpot!" He laughed and tested the bag to see if the Ziploc was working. It wasn't, so we got candy on the counter, some on the floor. He bent to get the stuff on the floor and stepped on a Tootsie Roll Pop that splintered and shot out from under his shoe. "Oops!" he said.

"Hold on," I said. "Freeze. Don't move."

"No. Hell, I got it," he said, lifting the foot, spraying brown candy crystals around. Right then the phone rang. He pointed at it. "Incoming," he said. "That's a pretty phone, too. That a decorator model?"

It was a yellow telephone. It came with the house, or something. Or Emily wanted it. I don't really remember.

Emily was calling to tell me the car was O.K. "It was low on oil, a quart low. There wasn't any on the stick when he pulled it out the first time, so I figured I'd torched it, but the guy says the new ones are all that way, I mean a quart low and they show nothing between those two little creases—you know what I'm talking about?"

"Byron is here," I said.

"Byron who?" she said. "You mean Byron Byron?"

"Yes," I said.

By this time Byron himself had made it across the kitchen and captured the receiver. "Byron to tower, Byron to tower," he said. "Come in with a friend. What's shaking, Em?"

He gave me a grin and a black-eye wink, then unwrapped a Tootsie Roll Pop he'd saved, a red one, and plopped it into his mouth as he talked. After a minute he put his hand over the mouthpiece and said, "I'm sorry about this mess here, Billy. Just lemme say hello to my sweet Em and I'll clean her right up." Then he screwed up his face as if thinking about that, jabbed a forefinger into the telephone mouthpiece, and said, "The mess, I mean. Not her."

I nodded my understanding and went for paper towels, listening to Byron's end of the conversation.

"You're too worried all the time, Em. You're off the beam, here. You got to stay low, flop around with the rest of us. Huh? Hey—but it's great to be here! I mean, I'm looking forward to sitting down with you, you know"— he gave me good front teeth, laughing at the joke he was making—"at the dinner table. Maybe you can cook me up that chicken thing you do, know the one I'm talking? Oranges and everything. Brown sugar? Boy, I've been missing brown sugar."

He took off wet clothes while he talked. The coat, then the shirt. He got the shoes off and was unbuckling his belt when he started doing kisses into the phone and pointed at it with his free hand to ask if I wanted to talk some more. I said I did and took the phone back from him while he got down to his shorts.

"Hi, Emily," I said. "It's me again."

"What's he doing?" she said. "What's he there for?"

"He looks great," I said. "Wet right now, and naked, but good. He has some kind of hair attitude, but I can't really tell. It's wet—he looks like a pop star."

"Pop star?" Byron said. He pulled the sucker out of his mouth and yelled, "We got designer hair. We got seventy-five bucks into the game right now." He pointed the red ball on the stick at his head. "The latest," he yelled, leaning so close to the phone that I could smell his breath. "The hair's hot!"

"It's hot," I said to Emily.

"It weeps for chicken!" he yelled.

When Emily got back an hour later Byron was on the couch in a pair of tennis shorts and a red polo shirt reading our movies-on-TV book. He was smoking a thin cigar with a wooden mouthpiece and talking to nobody in particular. "*Mr. Arkadin,*" he said. "A must-see—you ever seen that one, Em?"

She went right by him into the kitchen and started unpacking groceries. "Saw it," she said. "Starts with an unmanned aircraft circling a foreign capital, right? There's a lot of stucco in it."

Byron dropped the book, swiveled off the sofa, and trailed her into the kitchen. "You get me a surprise?" he said.

"Chicken," she said.

He did a quick circle, jamming both fists into the air one after the other, then danced around in a touchdown-style frenzy—kind of Mark Gastineau out of Martha Graham via Bob Marley. "Killer chicken," he said. "I eat the wings, I break the back, ya ya!"

Emily wasn't moved. She had on her career-woman outfit—tightly creased clothes, full-face makeup, jewelry—all slightly debloomed by the weather.

"And . . . that's not all," she said, pulling a package of Mallomars out of a sack. She did a little flourish with the cookies, then spun them onto the countertop next to Byron. "For the Mallomar man. You ate a hundred of these in one night, didn't you?" She turned to me. "Didn't Janie tell us he ate a hundred of these one time? They were fighting or something? Remember?"

I shrugged, although I did remember and I don't know why I didn't just say yes.

Byron groaned and rubbed his stomach. "God, I was crazy then. I must've been nuts. She was killing me about something or other, and then did the dinner thing, you know—" He did a mincing imitation of my sister that made her look like a bad TV homosexual. "Like what did I want for dinner right in the middle of this huge brawl we were having, and I said I wanted Mallomars and went out to the store and bought about forty packages and brought 'em back and dumped 'em all out on the table and sat there eating all night while she punched around on a salad with a tiny fork. Next day she told me I had the stink of Mallomars about me."

"You were looking for trouble," Emily said.

He grinned at her, something that was supposed to be conspiratorial, I guess, and said, "Still am." He must've thought the look I gave him was disapproving or something, because then he laughed and said, "Not really, Billy. I just said that to be interesting. Em understands, don't you, Em?"

She was busy working on the chicken, her back to us. "Sure," she said. "You're just talking, right?"

"Right," Byron said. "I'm a big talker."

"That's what we hear," Emily said. She has a way of saying things like that and making them seem, if not friendly, at least not terribly hostile.

I smiled at Byron, and he smiled back, the same smile as before, untouched. "Well," he said to me. "I suppose we're wondering what I'm doing in these parts." He took out a new cigar and lit up, rolling the thing between his fingers while he mouthed the smoke. In a minute he let it out and said, "That's a good question. I'm glad you asked me that, Billy. Honest."

He didn't get a chance to tell us then because the doorbell rang. I went to get it and it was Janie, my sister, standing on the stoop looking like she'd walked over from their place. She had on this huge coat, one of those thick, tan, winter jobs, good around Christmas time, and it was soaked, and her hair looked as if they'd just finished skull surgery on her and were trying to obscure the evidence. I hugged her, but then we got in the middle of this hug and she wouldn't let go, so I stood there looking at the rain falling off the edge of the roof and thinking that I'd probably like to hug her more if she weren't soaking wet. I felt guilty for thinking that, and for wishing she and Byron would just stay over at their house and have their fights alone, like everybody else, and then she said, "I love you, Billy. I really love you."

"Me too," I said, thinking how uncomfortable it was when somebody says they love you when you're not expecting it, or when you kind of take it for granted and wish they would too, and I wondered how many times in a life you say "Me too" to somebody who has just said they love you and then think that it isn't what you mean, that you love yourself too, that what you mean is that you love *her* too, or him, but that there isn't any quick way to say that, not in two words, anyway. That's the kind of thing I think about all the time—that, and wondering what the other person is thinking about, if the other person is thinking the same thing. "Byron is here," I said. I was trying to wedge my way out of the hug, but she was having none of it.

"Oh, Christ," Janie said, and she started crying. It was a very quiet kind of crying, she wasn't bawling, just kind of standing there with her arms locked around me and jerking like some kind of mechanical device having taken leave of its senses. I was trying to figure how to play the thing. Nobody'd told me anything—I mean, I knew we had a fight going on, but that's all I knew—so I was wondering what I should do next when Emily came out of the kitchen with her fist inside of a clean-plucked three-pound chicken.

She said, "Who is it, Billy?"

"It's Janie," I said. "My sister Janie."

Byron stuck his head out of the kitchen. "Why, howdee, little flower. How you doing? You following me around the country or something?" He moved across the foyer toward us as if to kiss her, but she was still hugging me and he pulled up short. "Oh," he said. "I forgot. We're having a tiff, right?"

Janie nodded at him, splashing her hair around. "We were. That was a couple of days ago. Before you left without telling anybody in the world where you were going or anything."

"I slipped down to Tampa," he said. "I was looking around. Checking it out. I was down there with Bruce Weitz."

She looked at him, a steady look, then rolled her eyes toward the ceiling. "O.K. I give up. Who's that?" she said.

"Belker," Emily said. "On TV. The ratty little guy on *Hill Street*."

"Only he ain't ratty," Byron said. "He looks like about a zillion. He had shoes on I'd be happy to drive around in. Had this jacket must've dropped him two thousand. Genuine chrome thread in there. Really."

"Byron hungers for the high life," Janie said. She'd finally let me go and had started hugging Emily, who could only hug back one-handed because of the chicken. You could tell it was bothering her. First she tried keeping it behind her back, then she tried a two-handed hug using just the arm of her chicken hand, but that didn't work, either, so the chicken was kind of dangling out there at the end of her arm, there at her side, as she hugged Janie.

"That ain't it," Byron said. He was scratching his stomach again. "The guy looks like a Swiss, know what I'm saying? Like they scrub him with white bricks every morning. I asked the desk girl what he was doing there and she said she didn't know, but that she didn't think he was *shooting*, like I'm some kind of rube's gonna get in the way if the man's there *shooting*, know what I mean?"

"He didn't like the desk clerk," Janie said.

I was worried about Emily and the chicken, so I put an arm around Janie and gave her a little tug, trying to break up the thing, and I said, "Well, it's like old home week around here. No clerks." I did another tug, this time toward the kitchen, figuring that even if I couldn't get them apart, at least in the kitchen Emily would have a chance on the bird. There were a couple of little spots of watery blood on the tile there in the foyer, but it wasn't too bad.

Janie took this opportunity to start hugging me again. She got me around the neck with one arm so she wouldn't have to let go of Emily.

"Hell," Byron said. "This girl was main line, only she was main line Tampa, which is like a gum-wrapper town out of Reno. I mean, Fitzgerald would've done stuff on her. Anyway—" he was keeping his distance, looking at the molding around the opening between the den and foyer "—there ain't anything there over four feet tall, know what I mean?"

"No, Byron," Janie said. "We don't know what you mean. Nobody ever knows what you mean." She finally gave up on Emily, though she still had me, and she pulled me over to the front door so we could get her shiny black duffelbag in off the stoop. This bag said "Players," like the cigarette, on the side. "Cars are taller than four feet, right?" she said when we got the door shut. "Don't they have cars in Tampa?"

"Sure," he said. "They got one. But it's this truck George Barris worked over in the fifties. Three foot eight."

She gave him an impatient smile.

"What I mean is—" Byron started to say, but as soon as he'd started she waved him off, which gave me a chance to get free, so I did.

"We don't care," she said, looking at me. "I don't care, anyway." She pointed to Emily and me. "Maybe they care, but I don't care what you mean. You could mean anything in the world and I wouldn't care." She shouldered the wet Players bag. "I had to wear this coat because I don't have the right kind of coat to wear at this time of the year in the rain because my husband's not such a knockout provider, if you know what I mean."

"I bought the coat," Byron said, talking to me and Emily, who had backed up all the way to the kitchen door.

"Yeah," Janie said. "My wedding present."

"There she goes," he said. "She's starting."

"Let me get this chicken put away," Emily said, waving the chicken hand at me. "Why don't you get Janie settled and then we'll all meet in the kitchen for a drink."

"She doesn't drink anymore," Byron said. "She's into health. If it doesn't have spinach in it she won't touch it."

"I know this great spinach drink," I said.

All three of them shook heads at me. I shrugged and grabbed Janie's bag. "Let's go, sis," I said. "We'll put you in the bedroom."

"Hang on," Byron said. "That's not my bedroom, is it?"

"You can have the office," I said. We'd made the third bedroom into an office that Emily used at home. We put the old couch in there.

"So what about my stuff?" he said. "I got it in the bedroom already. You gonna put her stuff in there with my stuff?"

Emily, who had gone around the corner into the kitchen and who had the water running in the sink, came back out drying her hands on three feet of paper towel and said, "So what's the deal? The luggage doesn't get along either?"

After dinner we stayed at the linoleum-topped table Emily had insisted we buy when those things were popular a couple of years ago. We sat around this table, the four of us, and stared at things. Everybody was staring in a different direction, like people in one of those realistic sculpture setups that you always see in *Time* magazine stories on modern art. Byron was watching something out the window over the sink. Janie was playing with blueberries in a bowl in front of her. Emily was reading the ads in the back of a boat magazine, and I was staring at the three of them, each in turn. We'd finished and we were just sitting there.

Janie said, "Where do these things come from, blueberries? I mean, where do they grow?"

"What are you talking about?" Byron said. "They grow on trees. Blueberry trees."

"Bushes," Emily said without looking up.

"You mean what state?" I said.

"No," Janie said. "I meant how. I mean, I've never seen a blueberry grow."

"Oh, that's great," Byron said. "Spent all your time watching watermelons, did you?"

"I've got it," Emily said. She circled a spot on the magazine page with a Day-Glo pink marker. "This is it—twenty-eight-foot Bayliner. Cheap."

"That's your K-Mart, Em," Byron said. "You'll be wanting a Bertram, be my guess. You can really hump a Bertram."

Janie said, "I'm sure that's just what she wants to do."

"La la la," Byron said.

"Why don't you leave her alone," Janie said. "If that's what she wants, that's what she wants."

"Oh, sure," Byron said. "Listen to Miss Genuine Fur-Lined Downy-Soft They-Said-So-on-TV the Third." He was checking the skin on his arms, twisting his arms forward and pulling the skin around his biceps. "Do people get warts at my age? I've been finding splotches." He turned around to show me what he was talking about. "See that?" he said. "That look a wart in embryo?"

There wasn't anything there—a little sun dot or something. I said, "Doesn't look bad to me."

"May this house be safe from warts," Janie said, making an ugly face at Byron. "He's worried about his age. He's going to be forty-one this year and he's getting all these tiny age spots. They're everywhere, they're all over him."

"She's happy about it," he said.

"I don't know what's wrong with it," Janie said. "Your life's half over. So what?"

He dropped his face into one hand, covering his closed eyes with fingers and shaking his head. "I was forced to marry her, wasn't I?" He jerked up and smiled at me. "No offense, Billy. She's a wonderful woman. It's a personality thing. She wants me to be a ninja."

Janie did a real sour look. "That's a joke about me watching karate movies on TV."

"What the hell is a ninja, anyway?" Emily said. "I've been hearing ninja-this and ninja-that for five years and I've got no clue. They wear a lot of black, right?"

"At least my brother doesn't whimper all the damn time because he's not Dan Pastorini or somebody. And he can keep a job," Janie said. "He has a career. He has a house—you know they've been in this house for eight years? And he's only thirty-something." She turned to me. "What are you now, Billy? Thirty-six?"

"Eight," I said.

"He's steady," Janie said. "That's what it's about."

Byron got up, adjusting the shorts again. "I know that it is," he said. "You're right. And it's a real nice house, too. I wish it was my house. I wish I'd been living here the last nine years."

An hour later I was lying in bed twitching the way I do when sleep won't come and my legs go numb—circula-

tion stops and I jerk around like a kid getting electrocuted, or what we thought electrocuted would look
like before we really saw it on TV. It drives Emily crazy
when I do it, so I got out of bed and went to the kitchen
and had Rice Chex. I was sitting there thinking about
Byron and my sister and how much trouble they were
having and I started thinking about me and Emily, and
how we got along pretty well. I mean, I started wondering if we were from another planet or something.

Then Janie and Byron came in wearing matching purple terrycloth robes. They were holding hands.

I looked at the clock on the stove but couldn't read it,
which is something I hate. It happens all the time. Even
in broad daylight the thing is hard to read. I said, "What
time is it there?" and motioned toward the stove.

Janie bent over. "How do you read this thing?" she
said. "Looks like it's four in the morning."

"It doesn't look like morning," Byron said. "Where
does it say morning?"

She gave him a playful little shove. "He's a detail guy,"
she said to me. "You know what I mean, right?"

"Twelve-twenty," I said.

Janie came over to the table and rubbed my shoulder.
"We just want to apologize, O.K.? We're sorry to be
messes, aren't we, Byron?"

"Yep," he said. He got a hand on my shoulder too.

They were both standing there beside me with hands
on my shoulder, and I was sitting there wishing I'd
stayed in the bedroom with Emily, thinking I should have
been smart enough to stay out of the kitchen. "Nothing
to worry about," I said, and I made as if to get up,
thinking that'd get rid of the hands, at least.

It didn't work. Byron came with me to the refrigerator, kneading my shoulder on the way. "You know how these things go," he said.

Well, I did know, but what I was thinking was how much I hate it when people that have no business touching you go around touching you all the time. But I figured I couldn't say that without hurting his feelings, so I let it go and opened the refrigerator, thinking the sight of leftovers might encourage him to forget me and go for the food.

"We got it all worked out in the bedroom," Janie said, coming up behind us. "We're going back to our place now."

"Tonight? You don't want to just sleep over?" I hated that. I felt like a bad guy, like no kind of brother at all. I reached into the refrigerator and got the black banana I'd been meaning to take out of there for a couple of weeks and handed it to Byron. "Toss this, will you?" I said. "It's Emily's, but she'll never get rid of it. She loves that banana like a son."

"What's wrong with it?" Byron said. He held up the banana, twisting it back and forth as if trying to find the flaw.

"Hell, it's perfect," Janie said, slapping his back.

I said, "There's steak here if you want steak."

Byron said, "Steak?"

"No thanks," Janie said, poking his shoulder. "We'd better go. It's just that we wanted to come in and apologize for hanging you up with our troubles. We always do it, don't we?" She'd backed up to the counter opposite the refrigerator and hoisted herself up on the countertop. "I didn't want you to worry about me."

"She thinks you spend all your time worrying about her," Byron said. He had the banana stripped down and half-eaten.

"I'm his little sister," Janie said. "Of course he worries, don't you, Billy?"

"I guess so," I said, but what I was really doing was looking on the bottom shelf in the refrigerator at a Ziploc bag of black beans, trying to remember when we'd last had black beans, and it seemed to me that it had been a while.

RESTRAINT

So I pass this woman in the hall. I'm leaving my room at the office, entering a corridor—it's a big office, three floors of this sudden building inside the loop, Philip Johnson or something. Architectonica. So here comes this woman—neat, got a nice suit, lemon-colored high heels, the usual—so I'm reading this memo I just got from Harriet Somes, our director of personnel, not really reading it but sort of holding it, and I look up as I pass the woman because that's what I always do, and . . . well, she's the most extraordinary three-dimensional construct I've encountered on the face of the planet in more than forty years without exception. Person—*person* I've encountered. So, anyway, I'm cool. I don't jump her, I just look, but I'm stunned like somebody's hit me with a floor lamp. Maybe I gawk some. I must seem like a goon to her—I mean, she's a young girl, I don't know, maybe twenty-two, twenty-one, seventeen, and she's not used to people looking the way I'm looking, not guys like me, three-piece guys. In the world of high finance we don't do mouth drops at our women in the hall—she has a right to be scared. Me, if I were her, I'd scream. But she's very relaxed. She's five nine, maybe a trace over that, to start with, and a little constellation of freckles perfectly deployed across the bridge of a nose from antiquity—unassailable, impeccable, prototype. It's got this curve to it, a rim at the nostrils—we're talking slight, barely perceptible, so fine it might as well be an optical effect, a passing condor emerging from a gray-green cloud bank casting a shadow that flickers through the mirrored exterior of our building and spins then, distorted and partial, up off the polished corridor floor, up into my eye. And the freckles, sweet and off-center, specks floating before her face, under the eyes, hovering like scout ships in advanced mathematical formation, fractals, ready for some mission into this soiled universe. Ready for Buster music. I don't know—it's like some scene from *Trancers*, full of New Age music, thunder volume, my redundant heart. A big thing. All backed by the eyes, guarded and protected, and yet clear as some glass flute melody lilting from out of nowhere over flat, distant grassland at last light on a disarticulated winter's afternoon in Montana, Wyoming, or some other state of that persuasion. These eyes are not blue, thank God. These eyes really aren't any color you'd recognize, or be able to name, and they are probably not any color that exists elsewhere in our planetary system, though in the universe, I am certain, the painstaking research assistant might locate a color proximate with respect hue, holding aside the paradox of texture. Of course, neither color, which in our radically diminished world of prepared things we'd call *brown*, nor texture, which remains elusive to verbal signification (i.e., can't be named), adequately suggests these eyes through which this young woman in the hall of our architecturally up-to-date corporate headquarters looks out upon a world that must seem to her a vile parody, the host site for yet another thin-walled condo community wherein lesser beings, cramped hopes whitened by grip, scoot hither and thither in search of niggling satisfactions. These eyes swell with hope and anticipation, ambition, crushing vulnerability, quick wit and vivid imagination, large heart, sweet disposition (which I had thought lost to the eighteenth century), all compressed in a two-dimensional array the size of a radio knob, of two thereof. I hasten to add that this is not all they swell with, but the merest sketch still some significance short of beginning to hint at the outline of a rendering of an artist's concept of a TV reporter's version—we got aces on the eyes. We got a fine nose, freckles in the proper number and distribution. We got tall. The hair's good—why, the hair's from the edge of Orion. Shines. Sways back and forth. Got a wispy aspect. Got secrets in it so marvelous as to rewhack the plexus. It's about a thousand colors, each so close to the next that the mordant eye can't tell the difference, only knows up there there's something otherworldly. Soft-looking hair, floats around at the telling moment, otherwise sits there like pure angel grace. It moves slowly, a rocking motion, coming toward you, then dodging away at the instant of maximum extension, in perfect sync with the smile, which gets you to the teeth—white like small wet cliffs, and straight enough to set your watch. No untoward lip-curling either—they retain their exquisite shape through the whole procedure, do these lips, they slide a little, opening into a gesture of welcome as if readying the private whispered report of some lovely indiscretion, something to brace the skin. There is, about this young woman, some quivering possibility I cannot place, a wonder that veils her like the barest morning mist, an interior surprise, a perfect curiosity regarding this time and place that strikes the onlooker more powerfully than icy Oriental scents. One is inclined, against one's will, to follow, to disregard caution and to throw, with all might, the self at the other. And yet I, in the cooling afternoon light of this outer corridor, restrain all still-operative nerve tissue, reduce and control motor behavior, and I do not, I am pleased to report, knock the young woman to the corridor floor, drag her by the gray-veined hair to my dark little post. No. I am an adult. I am a decent man. I grip a potted plant, lean inelegantly against a carpeted wall, gape like a monkey at the biggest banana ever to prowl up out of a tree, but I do not accost, maul, mash, whistle, or deliver myself of some gratuitous oral discharge apropos her stride, her skirt, her slight little ivory-shadowed calves, the taut muscles of which I can already feel swelling into my curled palm. No. I take what is given. As she passes I bathe in the fragrance of thousand-year-old lilacs on a stone path at misty dawn in Shanghai, and, when she turns the corner and leaves my sight, I return to my own boxy place where there is little to agitate the senses, sit in my gray vinyl chair, cock my feet on the round-cornered desk, and, lips pursed, eyes shut like vault doors, I count blessings, first health and family, then friends, and finally appliances, working my way from the large to the small.

RESET

People at the office assumed Ann and I had been having an affair for the five years she'd been working for me. We hadn't, though we hung around together all day, every day, and we fought and bickered and made fun of each other the way husbands and wives do, so I guess it's only natural everybody thought we were in some kind of love. We probably were, though we hadn't pushed it. Recently things had cooled off quite a bit between us. She was rarely around at lunch, and the daily play had turned a little more bitter than it had to be. Still, it was a shock when she came in to quit. She gave me ten minutes' worth of reasons—her recent divorce, from a professional golfer named Carl; that there weren't any good men around; how great it would be to get a new start somewhere; what fabulous job opportunities she'd heard there were in Texas. About halfway through the list I started feeling kind of lost, as if what I had to say, what I wanted, didn't matter at all—she had her mind made up. We'd talked about her leaving now and then, but it hadn't occurred to me that she'd really do it, and now that she was in front of my desk, on one foot, her pale-blue eyes high and bright, the irises clipped by the upper lids, and she was cool, clear and definite—well, I felt as if the bottom had dropped out.

I said, "I'm real sorry. I thought we'd just stay together. You know, onward and upward."

"Me, too," she said. She was looking down a lot.

I said, "Let me try that again. I don't want you to go. We're a team. We've been together a long time. Why do you have to quit?"

"It's just the way it goes," she said. "I really don't want to do it. I've been sweating this one for a long time. It's much worse, thinking about leaving here, than the thing with Carl. You helped me with that."

"Nope," I said. "I was clean, remember? I stood for patience and reconciliation."

"You wanted him out, didn't you?" she said. "I knew what you wanted."

People kept coming in congratulating her, asking questions about her plans. I didn't like it much, so I asked her to shut the door. She gave me a look, then closed it just enough so that the edge touched the jamb.

"I'm serious," I said. "I want you around all the time. I think about you."

"I think about me, too." She nodded, then took a breath and held it, exploding her cheeks like Dizzy Gillespie.

"Great," I said. Out the window some city workers in orange overalls were tearing up the street. There were ten guys out there working on a hole the size of a sink. They kept going over to their trucks for water or something.

"I don't like this," Ann said. "Doing this." She made a little wave at me and at the room, then stood there with her hands at her sides. She toyed with her mother's wedding ring on her right hand, rolling it around her finger with her thumb. Her mother had bigger fingers than she did. And then she sat down, folded her hands in her lap, and looked at her knuckles.

She was very still, upright in the blue chair facing my desk, the hands now quiet in her lap. Her skin caught the summer light in this fashion-magazine way, became luminous, delicate, soft. The look she gave me was about the loveliest thing I'd ever seen—fierce, full of determination.

"You're real pretty," I said.

She got up. "Hey! I'm trying," she said. "I'm giving you the A stuff." She opened the window. Our building is old and has windows that open. She crossed her arms over her chest and sniffed the air, watching the guys in the street. I went around the desk and stood beside her, smelling her hair. I always told her how nice she smelled, and she always laughed and said it was Dial.

"Maybe you don't have to do this," I said. "No kidding. It'll kill me if you go."

"That's weak," she said. She put an arm around my waist. "Anyway, you deserve to die." She giggled at this joke and then stared some more at the workers. After a couple of minutes she turned her head a little and said, "Wouldn't it be nice if you could make me stop? I mean, wouldn't that be something?"

Robin Romer, an account rep who worked on the other side of the office, poked open my door and asked Ann if she wanted to go out and celebrate. "You're going to Austin, right? Perfect town, great town." He stared out my window for a minute. "This place reminds me of a place my brother Desmond would like. He's over in Nam working up an import thing."

"He must be the interesting brother," I said.

Romer did a shrug and went right on. "Yeah, you know, the usual crap they bring in from places like that. Grass crap and stuff. Baskets. Those people can do baskets." He did a kind of leer at Ann. "I might go over there and learn the business, but first I've got some stuff to learn around here."

She patted his shoulder. "Mr. Romer has a problem with his chickens."

"Anyway," he said. "No point hanging around, is there?"

"Hey!" Ann said, hooking a thumb at me. "What about him? I have to take care of my Boss, don't I?"

"He's cool," Romer said. "Aren't you, Boss?"

He was a small man, always neatly tucked into a little suit, and I didn't like him. She used to make fun of him, but since the divorce she'd been making a lot of new friends, and he was one. A couple of days before, when I'd made some tasteless crack about Romer, she got mad and gave me a lecture on tolerance. I liked him less now that she was defending him.

I scratched two fingernails across my forehead. "I'm cool," I said.

"He can come with us," Romer said. "We'll loosen him up, show him a good time. We're going to Blood's." Blood's was a bar a block away in the basement of a butcher shop. People from the office routinely went there for drinks after work. I'd been a couple of times.

Romer swung out of my office, pivoting on the hand he had on the doorjamb, but no sooner was he out than he was back. "What's he going to do without you?" he said to Ann. "How will he function?"

"Rehire," I said.

She gave me a tight look, then smiled at Romer. "You can go now, O.K.? We'll be there."

He stayed gone this time, and Ann shut the door again and came around behind me. She traced the hair over my ears with her fingertips.

"I'm sorry," she said.

"You can pick 'em," I said.

"I picked you," she said. "First. Anyway, that's not what I'm talking about. I meant I'm sorry I'm so polite. I think maybe I've got a self-esteem problem. Let's go get the drink."

We went to the bar. Romer must have got lost along the way. We were the only people there from the office. It was dark and cold, and there were pockets of customers around. We got a corner table. While we waited for the woman to bring our drinks, Ann said, "My family used to take these holiday trips. Dad got bored with retirement and decided we needed quality time together. A couple years ago it was Florida—Gorilla World Headquarters, famous for the petting zoo."

"I love those places," I said.

"Me too, me too. They're so seamy. It's like you can barely believe them, know what I mean?"

I looked at the snack menu, which was a hand-done sheet in a plastic sleeve. I was wondering what she'd think of stuffed mushrooms.

"He was a priest," she said. "Episcopal. He really didn't like women very much. He was always putting them down, saying they'd do anything in a thunderstorm." She glanced at me, then checked the rest of the room.

"So," I said, craning toward the bar window. "What's the weather?"

"You're a mop," she said. She studied my face, her eyes doing a tiny box step. It was a way she always looked at me, something I figured was proprietary, something I liked.

"Thank you," I said.

She hunched over the edge of the table, looking earnest and innocent. "Why's somebody so upset? I mean, a girl'd think we were talking major love here, the way you carry on."

"We're talking," I said.

She toyed with the saltshaker, moving it in chess patterns on the checked tablecloth. First, the knight, then the rook. Our drinks came. Ann gave me a nice look while the woman was getting the napkins down, then watched her go and spun the ring. When the woman was out of the way she said, "So maybe I'll just stay here with you forever."

I said I thought that was a good idea.

Ann was on the phone when I stopped at her office door the next morning around nine. "Hey," I said.

She held up a finger telling me to wait a minute, then finished on the telephone. When she hung up she said, "You want coffee? I can get us some coffee."

"Not for me," I said. "I want love only."

"Got no love," she said. "You've got a choice of genuine emotion of unspecified type, ordinary friendship, or . . .

that other stuff. Any combination. But you're taking a ride on the love."

"Big offer," I said.

"We try," she said.

Her office was drab. She'd brought plants and a Diebenkorn poster, but the effort was halfhearted. The poster was still leaning against the wall, where it had been leaning for over a year. She held the point of her pencil while she watched me get into a chair across from her.

"It's personal," I said, reaching to close the door.

"I'm still going," she said.

"I know," I said. I couldn't get the door, and I was all twisted up—legs out in front, one over the other, body turned ninety degrees at the waist, left arm out at full length toward the door. My shoulders were perpendicular to her desk, and my head, which ought to have been facing the wall of her office, was twisted back toward her. "You probably don't recognize this body language," I said. "It's foreign. Dutch, I think it is. Colonial. Celanese, maybe."

"Celanese is a fabric," she said.

"That's what I mean." I shut the door, then sat straight again. "So. This is a great office. I like the poster—what is that?"

"Hard to believe?" she said, examining the mess she was making between her fingers with the pencil. Pretending to be tough was a routine. I played soft, she played hard. It was fun. It had always been fun, from the first day. I thought about that.

I said, "Can you go to Tennessee? I'm going to Tennessee today. Our client—Mr. Romer's client—Starlight,

Inc., wants a new headquarters, and they have, as you know, discovered Knoxville. Or someplace near Knoxville. I leave in an hour. You don't have to go. I just thought it'd be nice to have some company."

She nodded. "Company's nice. Is this, like, a date? I mean, twenty-third-century version?"

"I don't know," I said, drumming my fingers on my knee. I looked at the empty parking lot outside her office. It was empty because the entrance was blocked by the men working out front. "I guess. Maybe it's a bad idea."

"I didn't say no," she said.

"Thank God," I said. Then I held up my hands, smiled, tapped my head. "Sorry. The heart's saying what the brain wants unmentioned. I'm supposed to be playing close to the chest through here, right?"

"You're doing fine."

"Thank you," I said, picking a stick of gum out of the pack on her desk.

"There's a lot of thanking going on this morning," she said. "I don't like it. Makes me nervous." She put her feet on the corner of the desk closest to the window, away from me, and gave me a friendly smile. "Now, how long a trip we talking?"

I put the gum back. "Forty years, tops."

It was noon when we got to Vesco's Motor Lodge & Weekender, in a town called Review, Tennessee, outside of Knoxville. The registration desk was knotty pine, decorated at one end with an inflated heart tied to a straw. The owner was Charlene Vesco, a woman in her fifties, squat and mannish, with rough hands, short fingers, square-cut nails. She was some relation to the notorious Vesco, she told us, and her mother had run the Weekender in the fifties, when it was the Blue Ridge Motor Court. Charlene signed us in, complaining about a couple she'd just signed out. "They were some bozo individuals, I promise you. I hope and pray never to see them again crossing my line of vision." Charlene gave me the eye. "That's a joke, son. But don't you worry about it."

I smiled at her.

"He never worries," Ann said. "He's worry free."

The motel was eighteen wood-frame bungalows bunched on two acres next to a stream the brochure called "Vesco Falls," though no falling of more than six inches was anywhere in evidence. Up the hill behind this place, stuck up in the trees, there was a plywood flamingo that must once have been painted but was now plain, weathered, streaked with pink at the edges.

Charlene caught me looking out the window at the sign. She said, "I was doing that in '62, when I took over. I figured to go it, you know, tourist art—birds on the ground, the whole thing. So then I started hanging around with the sign guy—he wasn't local—and, well, we did a one eighty on the plans." She winked at Ann and handed over the keys. "I'm guessing you understand, right?"

"Right," Ann said.

I was in number ten, surrounded by tall pines. I had two rooms and a kitchen the size of a confessional. Ann was in seven, in a tiny clearing thirty yards away. The bungalows were war era, white, trimmed brown around the windows and at the eaves.

We put up our stuff and then I called Ketchum, the

town-council guy we'd come to see about Starlight. The
first thing he wanted to know was if Ann was with me—
he'd talked to her a lot on the telephone. I told him she
was. "Then I'm buying lunch," he said. "You had lunch?
We got motel or drive-in. Or local color, but it's kind of
sticky."

I chose the latter and he told me how to get to a place
called Raindrop's, and then we hung up.

Ann and I drove into town, following his directions to
the letter. At a stoplight we pulled up next to a giant
Volvo driven by a guy with hair combed to a point in
front. He grinned, then dropped his visor, and looked
into a mirror on the back.

"Pretty damn thrilling," Ann said, seeing the guy.

We watched him work his teeth. Then his mustache.
Then he brought out some tiny scissors. I turned away,
but he was hard to ignore. When I looked again he was
on the telephone *and* working the scissors. He was laughing into the receiver.

"Maybe you could get a job with him," I said.

"Will you stop?" Ann said.

We followed the Volvo right to Raindrop's. The driver
turned out to be Ketchum.

We spent the afternoon with him. I'd hoped to be able
to get by on lunch alone, but he was so happy to see
Ann, and she was so nice about it, that at five he was still
showing us the sights. We got to see the tar pits, the train
depot, the rushing brook that sliced the town in half. We
saw the land south of downtown that he had a piece of.

"I can get you in on this," he said. He did a slow-
motion punch on the top of my arm. "Blind, of course.
No problem."

"Looks mighty handsome," I said.

He went back to Ann, slinging an arm over her shoulder. "We're going for the whole 'new town' thing," he said. "Maybe work out a lake over beyond the bank. Wipe all that out, of course." He waved at a two-block stretch of single-story brick buildings. "Nuke those dudes and swing back with the wood-siding thing, you know? Very upscale, West Coast—nothing modern, just nice middle-of-the-road shops, family-orientated."

Ann was smiling hard, pointing some.

I took a nap when we got back to the motel, then cleaned up and went to find Ann. She was with Charlene in the office. They were drinking coffee, sitting at one of the three tables in the alcove that was the Weekender restaurant. They were looking at a magazine open to a picture of a model with bruisecolored cheeks, black lips, eye sockets like anodized aluminum. She was wearing a lace top, a zebra skirt with a red belt, burgundy stockings, shoes with silver flames. The jewelry was big wood, and the hair was stiffed up in a wedge.

"Well, she ought to be out trying wieners," Charlene said. She smacked a knuckle on the open magazine. "I'm telling you."

I said, "She's probably real lovely." I had come up behind them and was leaning over Ann's shoulder.

"Well, looky here," Charlene said. She gave me a pat on the shoulder. "You want some eats? Just don't ask for no lobster bisque, hear? I ain't seen lobster in forty years. You want something like that you're gonna roll on down the road."

"I asked for lobster bisque," Ann said.

"That's true," Charlene said. "Now, if you want toast, I can handle toast."

"The toast is great," Ann said.

Charlene, already on her way toward the kitchen, stopped and did a suspicious look.

"Honest," Ann said. "It's incredible toast, really." She started to cross her heart with a finger, but stopped halfway through.

The phone was ringing in the next room. Charlene did an eye roll and cut across toward the registration desk. In a minute she was back, dragging the telephone with her. She got about halfway to us before she ran out of cord.

"It's your office," she said, wiggling the receiver at me.

I took the phone. "Hello?" I said.

It was Romer, calling to tell me Starlight had changed its mind. "I guess you'd better forget it," he said.

"Are you sure?"

"Sure I'm sure," he said. "What, I'm making it up? We just got a call ten minutes ago."

"O.K.," I said. "Thanks."

"Hang on," he said. "Uh . . ." There was a pause, and that closed sound you get when somebody on the other end of a telephone call puts a palm over the mouthpiece. Then he was back. "Listen," he said. "Is your friend Ann around there?"

I said, "No, she's not around. I think she's at the pool."

"That's all right," Romer said. "I guess I'll catch up with her later. Don't worry about it. You O.K.?"

"Fine," I said. I hung up and carried the phone through the arched doorway and put it on the desk, then sat down again. I started rubbing my eyes, because the lids were clinging to each other, but then it seemed like I couldn't stop rubbing. Finally, Ann tugged my arm. "Are you O.K.?" she said. "What's the deal on the phone?"

"Starlight's down the tubes," I said.

"No kidding?"

"That's it," I said. "Romer asked for you." I was working on my eyes again. "You have a change of heart or anything?"

She pulled away, reaching for her coffee mug.

"Sorry," I said. "It's just that I dreamed about you in my nap. We were in a parking lot. There wasn't anything there but this pink asphalt and the blue sky. We were naked, lying out there. You didn't have any legs, and you had one arm. I mean, you had the legs and the other arm, but you'd taken them off or something. I asked why and you said you were saving them."

She sighed and dropped her head into her hands.

"Yeah," I said. "I know. I didn't want to dream it, either. Tonight I'm going to dream about bowling." I looked at her eyes, which were tired and watery.

Charlene came through the kitchen door with a ten-inch stack of toast. She noticed Ann's eyes right away, then mine, and stopped short of the table, pulling the plate back and to one side as if she might withhold it. "What've we got here? We got an outbreak of iritis? We can probably fix that."

"Contact trouble," Ann said. She shut one eye and swiveled around, looking for the ladies' room.

"Mine are fine," I said, and when the toast was on the table I picked a piece off the stack. The toast was as thick as a paperback, crisp at the edge, collapsed in the center.

Charlene pointed Ann toward the front office, then stood in back of me looking out the window, her hands crimping on my shoulders. When the door shut behind us, Charlene said, "Now, you be good to her, hear?"

"Yes'm," I said. "I'm trying."

"No . . . I'm serious," Charlene said, giving me a squeeze. "She's bananas about you. Any fool can see that."

I craned my neck, looking up at her.

She nodded at me. "Sure is," she said. Then she popped my forehead with a finger in a way that was friendly but hurt like hell. "Just be nice. Give her what she deserves."

We went to dinner at a drive-in that was once a Dairy Queen, now a local outfit called Princess Snack. There were hand-painted drawings of snacks all over this place. And princesses. A young girl in red satin took our order and brought the food. We sat in the car and ate. Neither one of us had much to say. I watched the cook and the cashier and the girl carhop mill around inside the building. They were mechanical, the way they kept repeating the same movements, the same gestures. Watching them, I got angry about Ann leaving.

I said, "I hate it when you're polite."

She raised her eyebrows. "Did I miss something?" she said.

"You were real nice to Ketchum and I hated it."

"I see," she said, drawing it out while she refolded the tissue on her hamburger. "It's going this way, is it?"

I looked out the window.

"My guess is that Ketchum's not the problem," she said.

"Right," I said. "I don't know why you like all these

other people better than me. Why you have to leave."

"I explained that," she said.

"Yeah, I know," I said. "But we get along, don't we? We have a good time. It's not so bad."

"Days are good," she said. "Nights aren't."

"They might get better," I said. "Who knows?"

She sighed, and we both watched employees for a while. The cook must have been a basketball fan. He kept doing sky hooks when he was flipping the patties.

Finally, Ann said, "Why don't we just have a nice time, huh?"

I started to say something about how it was hard to have a nice time with her departure looming, but as I was talking I was gesturing with my hamburger and I lost the meat. It slipped out of the bun and fell down around the foot pedals. I had to scrounge for it, and it broke in two when I found it. I got it off the carpet and out onto the tray, and when I turned around Ann was sitting there grinning at her lap.

"What?" I said.

"Nothing," she said.

I smiled at her and pointed at her hamburger. "You finished with that?"

She handed it to me. "You still want it?"

I squinted at her when she said that. A line of pink light reflected from the restaurant sign cut across her forehead, over the bridge of her nose, down her cheek. We sat still for a minute. Then I took a bite of the hamburger she'd given me and I grinned. "Why, sure," I said. "On the something-is-better-than-nothing principle."

She reached over and messed with my shirt collar, then

sat back and looked out the car windshield. "That's sort of one of my favorites," she said. "The other one I like pretty much is better late than never."

"Yep," I said. "I'm crazy about that one."

Later, when I couldn't sleep, I got a glass of tap water and stood at the front window of my bungalow looking at the lit-up grounds. I'd only been there a minute when I saw Charlene Vesco creeping across the grass.

I opened the venetian blinds. Charlene went up on the porch of Ann's bungalow and tested the screen, then stood there moving foot to foot, scanning the property, her back to the door. She patted her hair a couple of times, getting it into place. I checked my watch. It was almost four. When I looked outside again Charlene was gone. Nothing moved for a while, and then Ann's door opened and there was Ann, barely visible through the screen. She had on shorts and some kind of big shirt, and she was wearing her glasses. She hated her glasses. Her arms were crossed over her chest at first, but then she opened them, holding the edge of the door with one hand, rubbing her thigh with the other. She was just looking around. In a minute she pushed the screen and came out onto her porch. She sat on the steps. I watched for a long time. There were shadows all over the place, and there was moonlight. I filled up my glass and pulled a chair to the window, propping my heels on the sill. I stared at the tree trunks, and the flat, nearly iridescent lays of grass. There was something set and fearsome about the scene, like a little tableau at the start of a Hitchcock movie: mist drifting through, water sparkling, lights high up in the pines—and Ann, in the clearing, on her steps. Two cars rolled by almost silently, almost in tandem, on the narrow road in front of the property. My window shined. I studied the scene outside my window. I tried to see the future.